Like Printing Money

A technological crime novel set in Baltimore

R.A. Cramblitt

BC Publishing Inc.

Cover design: Ross Brandt
Author's photo: Mark Reich

ISBN: 979-8-9854742-2-0 (eBook)
ISBN: 979-8-9854742-3-7 (paperback)

www.racramblitt.com

Prologue

Bernard Jamal woke up in the trunk of a large car, his left temple throbbing and ass aching. He reached up and his hand rebounded off the felt roof of the trunk, a jolt of alarm reverberating through his 6' 6" frame.

There was little that Bernard feared. Growing up in East Baltimore, he'd seen a man die on a sidewalk, his chest spurting blood from a shotgun wound the size of a baseball. He'd heard the sounds of gunfire reverberating nearly nightly in the black air; given a wide berth to skinny men in sagging jeans jumping out of their skins on crank; watched as fellow teenagers were braced against cop cars for the crime of walking through their own neighborhood late at night.

He'd been a thrill seeker as a kid and teenager, cruising the streets with his boys looking for things to climb. Rusty fire escapes leading to the top of an early 20th century apartment building, pedestrians looking like figurines in those train gardens that the city fire stations stage for the holidays. In the dead of night climbing the scaffolding surrounding one of the few remaining water towers in the city, sneakers crunching on the gravel-covered roof. Buzzed on MD 20/20 in the suburbs, the night air bristling against their cheeks, scaling a microwave tower and gazing at the city lights to the south, all the way to the diffused glow of M&T Stadium, where the Ravens were playing Monday Night Football.

Fearless he was, unless thrown into a dark, enclosed space like the one he was now lying in, sprawled diagonally, his head in the far right corner and feet bumping against the ledge at the front of the trunk.

When he was five, Bernard visited an older cousin who lived south of the city. He fell in with the cousin's gang, exploring a junkyard filled with abandoned treasures, including an old refrigerator that his cousin's buddies dared him to step into. He climbed into the space that was just big enough to contain him. When he curled up inside, they closed the door. Instant darkness. He pushed against the door to get out, but they held it shut on the other side, making their voices sound increasingly distant and tamping their feet in place to simulate walking away. They started calling out at incrementally lower volumes, as if fading into the distance: "Later, Bernie," "See ya tomorrow," "Have a nice day," "Don't let the bed bugs bite." Laughing brutally. When they finally relented and stepped away from the door, Bernard leaped out of the refrigerator and attacked his cousin, tackling him at his waist and raining blows on his head and stomach. His cousin knew he deserved it and let Bernard hit him until the smaller boy was exhausted. They picked themselves up and walked to the corner store, where his cousin bought Bernard an ice-cream sandwich. But Bernard never got over that fear of being helpless in a dark space where you couldn't spread your arms and legs; where it felt as if your breath was being spirited away.

What were the odds that Bernard would be revisiting that horror as a 32-year-old man, a man who has made millions for shareholders as a venture capitalist and stands to make millions more with his current investment?

1

It was 8 p.m. on a Tuesday night at the headquarters of a 3D printing company in Locust Point, a peninsula at the mouth of Baltimore's Inner Harbor. At the tip of the peninsula is Fort McHenry, famous for repelling an onslaught from British troops in the War of 1812, a battle that inspired America's national anthem.

There was a new type of history unfolding in the company's laboratory called the nightshift. Two engineers and a former executive are staking their claim on a product that could change the world, for better or worse depending on one's perspective

The three men are composed but excited as they pull the prototype from the 3D printer and vacuum away the excess material. What they are doing has never been done before, but they have confidence. Not the confidence of idle dreamers, but one borne of experience, skill and the ability to produce new product iterations faster than ever before, thanks to 3D printing technology that speeds the design-to-manufacturing cycle.

The prototype coming out of the 3D printer tonight is a complex configuration designed as one part, with no assembly required except insertion of a small, flat battery. One of the engineers designed the prototype and the other developed the materials used for 3D printing, leading to a device with unique characteristics: a small footprint, light weight, nearly silent operation, and speed and power that seem to defy physics. The former executive is the money man behind the operation.

The designer is in his late 20s, quiet but assured. He knows he's special and has been recognized as such throughout his university years and his subsequent working career. He has an ego, but it doesn't need outside stroking. His partner, the materials specialist, is a few years older but appears younger. He's shy in formal social situations, but lets his inhibitions loose on a Friday night. The money guy has the bluster of a man born of privilege; a man who thinks he knows everything about anything. He isn't shy about telling anyone they are wrong.

There's an air of pent-up energy, as all three sense this is the night, the way a baseball pitcher can feel a big game coming on when his warm-up pitches behave exactly as they should.

2

Buck Boyd was jobless and holed up in a decrepit house in Curtis Bay, in the southern part of the city. He had been fired from his most recent construction job after failing a drug test. Nothing about his on-job performance suggested a firing to Buck's knowledge. He simply failed a mandatory test.

In Buck's mind, the nation was built by men fueled on alcohol and drugs. He remembered the story of the Mohawks that built the Empire State Building and the Chinese who built the railroads. He was certain they were never drug tested. The NFL doesn't test players for weed anymore. A responsible white man like Buck takes a few tokes at night to wind down and he's out of a job.

Buck thought drug testing was dictated by the elites who never worked a hard day in their lives. Never ached so badly they had to self-medicate to sleep. A white man used to be able to make serious money doing physical work, with nobody butting into what he did at the end of the day. His father and grandfather ground out a good living over three decades each at Bethlehem Steel. Showing up and doing your job were the only expectations. That era had passed by the time Buck was old enough to work full-time.

Jackie had told him that Beth Steel was back in business, but when Buck googled it, he saw that it was 500 jobs and they were going to be making windmills. *Fuckin' windmills!* Buck thought it all came back to the smartasses saying that oil and gas are no good anymore. *Five hundred jobs!* More than 30,000 worked at Beth Steel at its peak. And there was GM, Glenn Martin, Westinghouse. Buck looked it up: In 1950, Baltimore had nearly a million people in the city. It was the sixth largest city in the country; now it's 30th and sinking fast. At least the governor was keeping the city from infecting the rest of the state, although Buck didn't blame Garrett and Allegheny counties from wanting to secede. But leave Maryland for West Virginia? Half the white people in Maryland came here to escape West Virginia.

Unlike those losers thinking they'll wait for things to get better, Buck has a plan, and it starts tonight, providing that Jackie doesn't fuck it up, which is a big providing. Jackie Reynolds, Fuckup at Large. Large all right—Buck tells everybody that the last time Jackie was weighed was at the heifer competition at the state fair; no other scale goes high enough. Buck likes to bullshit people, but Jackie is a big boy. Big enough to pick up the back end of a Mini Cooper. Big enough to put cuffs on Bernard Jamal, who's now going to pay; pay for having an easy life as a venture capitalist, whatever the fuck that is, without having to trudge through the piles of shit that faced Buck every fucking day. Everything handed to Jamal because he could put a ball through a hoop for four years in college.

3

Jackie told Buck about Bernard Jamal after he saw an article in the *Baltimore Sun* about his venture capital firm funding a 3D printing company that promised to bring back manufacturing to America. The article called it reshoring.

Jackie went to University of West Baltimore for two years on a football scholarship, where he knew about Jamal but never socialized with him. That was before Jackie busted up his knee and got hooked on the oxy. He could hold down a job for a while, but then the pain would haunt him at night until he'd go sleepless for three or four days. He'd finally pass out one morning before work and sleep for another couple of days, leaving the job behind. He'd take the oxy again and get back on the wheel, working for a few months, staving off the pain, and then succumbing again.

He didn't think life could turn on him this way. He'd been a star in high school, not major university material, but good enough to hold down the all-important offensive left tackle position—known as "the blind side"—for a University of West Baltimore team that won its conference and went to the Old Bay Chesapeake Bowl in his sophomore year. He had graduated from Poly High with honors and was doing okay academically at UWB, going for a mechanical engineering degree when that asshole freshman trying to prove himself hit him from behind and his knee collapsed, rupturing his ACL. He had surgery to reconstruct the ligament with one harvested from a cadaver donor. He did all the rehab work and looked set to resume his career nine months later when the knee gave out again on a routine left sweep in a preseason game. This time it took the heart out of him. He left school for good, stepping up his daily dosage of oxy to relieve the pain.

Oxy doesn't come cheap and once you're on that boat, needing increasing doses to keep functioning, you're at its financial mercy. Jackie worked two jobs to support his habit, construction during the day and the nightshift as a security guard. He slept about five hours a night and was always tired. Nowadays, when he looked in the mirror he didn't see that bright, unlined, baby face with the dimples that charmed girls in high school. Staring back at him was the wizened face of his long-lost alcoholic father, who skipped town for good when Jackie was 15, leaving he and his mother scrambling to survive.

There were no women in his life now and he discovered that he didn't miss them. Not even Kathryn Lowry, his high school sweetheart who stuck with him through the first year of rehab and finally left him after he smashed a hole in her apartment wall. She was like football; something Jackie had to put in the rearview mirror. He actually felt that he was lucky in one way: He had no real responsibilities to others. No wife or girlfriend. No parents to support. No kids. He was an island; a barren, infertile island perhaps, but one that belonged to him alone.

The one thing he could count on now was people thinking he was dumber than he was. Always underestimating him. That's how he could steal from the cash register of a Fells Point bar without them catching on for seven months. They didn't suspect the silent, hulking, seemingly loyal guy who showed up every day and doggedly worked his shift. He wasn't greedy; he took what he needed and when he was fairly flush, he didn't take anything more. It would have worked out fine if the pain didn't start escalating and the sleep wouldn't come, leading to a series of missed shifts.

Now it's this thing with Buck. Something that might give them a cushion for once in their lives. He didn't know what Buck wanted to do with his money, but Jackie thought he'd go to Mexico or Uruguay, someplace where weed and drugs were cheap and he could wean himself back to the person he was, slowly, like a long-term rehab.

Jackie had nothing against Bernard Jamal, but he was the one standing between himself and that dream place.

4

Bernard Jamal was sitting in his office, reviewing the latest financial figures in his investment portfolio when Prisha Kapoor called. He had been thinking of wrapping up early and stopping home before going to Farley Recreation Center for his weekly pickup basketball game. Now he had to change plans.

Prisha was the chief financial officer for 3Make, the 3D printing company Bernard's firm was helping finance. She wanted to meet him at the Formosa Club, a tiki bar with small tapas-like dishes in Canton. Bernard knew that Prisha didn't drink so the request was odd to him. When he asked if anything was wrong, she replied "I can't say at this point" in the type of even voice his grandmother would use when something bad happened and she didn't want the children to get upset.

Bernard had wanted a snack before playing ball anyway, and the bar was not too much out of the way, so he agreed to meet Prisha at 5:30, giving him time to have a couple of small plates, maybe a beer or glass of wine, then drive to the gym for the typical start time at 7.

When he arrived at the Formosa, the maitre d' greeted Bernard as if he was expected and took him to a back room lined with private booths with curtains drawn. Bernard parted the curtains to see Prisha with what looked like a club soda in front of her, consulting her phone. Prisha was a quiet, hard worker, who could recall any bit of financial minutia about 3Make within seconds from that rapid-response database inside her head.

Bernard scooted into the other side of the red-leather-covered banquette opposite Prisha, folding his hands on the mahogany table. Prisha is stunningly beautiful and it felt uncomfortable for Bernard, legs as long as Prisha's entire body, to sit so close to her. He tried to lean back a bit, but the seat of the banquette didn't allow much room. Her coal-black hair was layered in bangs just above her eyebrows and flowed like lacquer down the middle of her back. Her skin was darker than his and seemed to be illuminated by subtle lighting coming from within. He reached across the table and took her tiny hand in his.

"Good to see you, Prisha. Come here often?"

She smiled weakly and shifted in her seat.

"Not my usual place of business," she said, her voice cracking at the end. Bernard hadn't seen that kind of tentativeness in her. She had a soft voice, but when she spoke it was always clear and confident.

"OK, so this is business. What's up? Please don't tell me you found another opportunity."

Competition for young financial people with experience in start-ups was fierce and Bernard had no doubt that Prisha was the target of multiple recruiters. She was only 28, but had already been in key financial positions for two companies that had been sold for a combined three billion dollars. That kind of success rate makes people take notice. Prisha could probably work anywhere she wanted, and it was a tribute to the potential of 3Make's technology and the tenacity of Bernard's recruiting that she was working for about two-thirds of the salary she could earn at another company. The key was the company shares she held, which could potentially be worth tens of millions.

Prisha folded one hand on top of the other and breathed out, her green eyes boring into Bernard's brown ones.

"Do you know about what they call the nightshift?"

"I didn't know they called it that, but Roland told me that some of the engineers were doing experimental stuff on the side at night. He didn't say exactly what, but that it could have some commercial potential."

Roland Hines was the founder of 3Make and now a technical advisor, pulling in a couple of million plus a 10-percent share of the company for devising an engineering plan and sitting in on meetings twice a month. The day-to-day technical work was led by Bill Christenson, the first engineer hired by Roland when he started the company.

"I'm uncomfortable with the secrecy, Bernard."

"Why are you concerned? Is it costing too much? Too much overtime or use of material, machinery or power?"

"At first it was that; more expenditure than budgeted. I talked to Bill about it, and he attributed it to supply chain problems, which are certainly an issue. But when I pressed him about what they were doing and the potential value to the company, he waved me off."

"Waved you off?"

"Basically said it was none of my business. But Tuesday night I stayed late preparing the quarterly financial report and heard a lot of yelling from the nightshift lab. It sounded like a celebration. I tried to enter the lab, but didn't have the entry code to the door. I rang the bell five or six times and finally a guy came to the door, opened it a crack and said that he was sorry for the noise, they were just messing around. I asked if I could come in and look around, but he closed the door and came back a few minutes later saying he'd called Bill and Bill had said that I wasn't authorized to go into that area."

Bernard ran his hand through his afro and rubbed the back of his neck.

"I can see where you'd be concerned, Prisha. Let's keep this to ourselves for now. I'll talk to Roland to see if he knows anything. I'm hoping there is an easy explanation. Thanks for bringing it to me; I appreciate your trust."

"You are the one who brought me on, and our investors have a lot of money riding on this, so I thought you should know." She paused for a few seconds, taking a deep breath.

"There's one more thing. When I went out to the parking lot that night? I saw Spencer Ohtari walking toward his car."

5

Charlaine Pennington watched the elegant Indian woman stride across the parking lot of 3Make, swinging what looked like a Tory Burch tote bag. She beeped the car door open and swung inside, flashing well-toned brown legs wrapped in a mid-knee-length pleated skirt. The skirt was black and it was topped with a cream-colored blouse and a boiled wool red jacket cinched at the waist.

The woman, named Prisha Kapoor, was driving a dark green Audi R8, a 2018 if Charlaine were to guess. Charlaine knew her cars, having worked for a spell at Prime European Imports in Reisterstown. If she had her way, she'd be in a Porsche Macan, but the PI gig made her err on the side of inconspicuous, as much as a gracefully curvy Black woman with incandescent facial features could make herself look. Today, she was in a loose track suit and a Baltimore Ravens cap. She was driving what her partner Joy called the Libmobile, a 2011 Subaru Forester with 80,000 miles on the odometer and probably tens of thousands more in real life.

She'd gotten her current gig six years ago via Joy, who had an ex-boyfriend from her straight days whose uncle had started an investigation agency that first handled insurance claims and then evolved into the edgier domestic and business stuff. The uncle, Tony Mancuso, started the agency with just himself and a secretary, but word spread about Tony's myriad skills and contacts. Simply put, Tony knew people and how to get results. Best of all he had discretion, and clients with no desire to know what went into the sausage. Tony wouldn't have told them anyway, as he classified his working methodologies as tricks of the trade or "proprietaries" in Tony's singular lexicon.

Charlaine filled the one big gap in Discreet Investigations Inc.'s staff: A Black woman operative in a city where Blacks are the majority. Tony questioned at first whether Charlaine could blend into the background like a PI has to, as she looked like what he called a "glam girl" in their first meeting. But Charlaine left the interview, went into the ladies' room with the bag she carried, washed the makeup from her face, changed into gray sweats, the Ravens cap, and dirty-looking Skechers sneakers and returned to the office, pushing a plastic trash can on wheels in front of her. The receptionist didn't blink as Charlaine slumped over the trash can and shuffled wearily into Tony's office. Tony glanced up at her and asked "Where's Cassandra today?" before the penny dropped. He hired her then and there and she's steadily moved up the ladder within DII.

Her first assignments were typical divorce stuff, husband stepping out on his wife or vice versa. Then came a couple of fraud cases she helped crack. She'd studied finance at community college and was as comfortable with a spreadsheet as she was following a person of interest on the Baltimore Beltway.

She showed up at her first DII Christmas party with Joy, a short, porcelain-skinned woman who favored Joan Jett, attitude included. Joy had helped teach Charlaine how to meld into the background, which she learned in junior high to avoid hazing from bigger, more mature girls. It helped when the girls found out she had a black belt and a temper.

Charlaine liked to know the particulars of an assignment so she could do her research and sink into her role, but this time Tony was tight-lipped about what she was to do and why she was doing it. She didn't like it, but figured it was Tony's obsession with "secretuities" and "maintaining confidentials."

It was Charlaine's second day on the assignment and she couldn't imagine what Prisha might have done or be in the process of doing. Tony only said that she might be "devolving secrets of a corporal nature." Charlaine trusted Tony for the most part but was skeptical about this young Indian woman being under suspicion. She didn't know much about Indians, but she kept up on white-collar crime and didn't think she'd ever seen an Indian woman involved in any type of spying, embezzlement, disclosure of trade secrets, or any of those other crimes that typically involved white males. Prisha had to be wealthy, as Charlaine had read her profile on LinkedIn and it documented the companies she helped go public and their net worth at the time. She was also married to a man high up on the engineering management chain for a promising start-up. Prisha was driving a $200,000 car and the clothes on her back and her pumps probably set her back five grand or so, but if she was making the typical salary for her position, none of her possessions, as far as Charlaine knew about them, were a financial stretch.

Aside from Prisha being an unlikely suspect, Charlaine wondered why anyone would sell secrets or embezzle from a company. It was a mug's game to her. You know you're going to get caught sometime; it's just a matter of when. But, she knew that people got away with it more often than is reported because companies don't want to be embarrassed about their poor security precautions. Several clients had told her as much, saying they wanted the perps to be uncovered by DII not so they could publicly prosecute, but so they could part ways quietly. It was the modern equivalent of a sheriff escorting the gunslinger out of town in the dead of night.

Prisha was now taking a right onto President Street and heading for Aliceanna, where she took a left, likely heading to Harborplace East, Fells Point or Canton. She definitely wasn't heading home, since she lived in Roland Park, and would have driven north on the Jones Falls Expressway or Charles Street from 3Make's headquarters in Locust Point. Charlaine followed from a car behind as the Audi stayed on Aliceanna in heavy traffic through Fells Point, bearing right on Boston Street alongside the outer harbor and taking a left on Hudson into the heart of Canton.

Prisha pulled into a parking garage and found a space on the second deck, Charlaine on her tail in the Subaru. Charlaine waited until Prisha was about 30 yards ahead of her and followed until she entered the Formosa Club. Charlaine knew the place was a hip spot and she would call attention to herself in the loose-fitting sweat suit, the Ravens cap, and Skechers. She turned and doubled back to the car, where she transformed into a long-haired, impeccably dressed Black business woman, no longer such a rarity in a place like Canton, which was now headquarters for bars, restaurants and nightclubs where even the Ravens hung out.

Charlaine settled on a stool at the bar with an empty seat beside her, as if she was waiting for someone to join her. She liked the vibe of the place. Red-lacquered bar, a DJ playing quiet jazz, everybody animated after a day of work. She reminded herself that she and Joy needed to go out more often—she followed people into places like this but never enjoyed them herself when off-duty. Come to think of it, there really wasn't much of a thing called off-duty for her.

Charlaine ordered a Pinot Noir and looked around for Prisha. She didn't see her in the bar area, but knew there was a back room at the Formosa, with open tables and private banquettes where you could draw the curtains. She settled in and like most of the singletons at the bar began scrolling on her phone.

When she looked up, the thing she dreaded was standing in front of her, nearly rubbing her knees with his plump thighs. He was one of a legion: White sales guy, probably a fullback or linebacker in high school, now filling into middle age in mostly the wrong places. He wasn't half bad if you overlooked the slightly bloated face and the red veins blossoming on his nose, attesting to the fact that he's a perennial happy hour attendee. He brushed back his hair with his hand, no doubt proud of it, still thick and blond, pushed up into a nice wave in front.

"Mind if I take this seat?"

"I'm expecting my boyfriend, but you can keep it warm until he arrives."

"Lucky guy. Can I make an observation?"

Oh shit, here we go thought Charlaine. If she had a dollar for all the times…

"I guess, as long as it's about the weather or Lamar Jackson."

He raised his eyebrows, but plowed on doggedly.

"I'm sure you hear this all the time, but you favor a certain movie star. Can you guess who?"

"You're right, I do hear it all the time, but I don't even like Gwyneth Paltrow."

Again with the eyebrow bit. Must have worked for him at some point.

"Funny line, but I was actually thinking of a beautiful Black woman. The one from that Tarantino flick."

"You mean Pam Grier? No way. Her tits are much bigger than mine and my ass is a lot bigger than hers. Now, if you'll excuse me, I just got an important text from work."

"I can wait."

"I'm sure you have all the time in the world, but I don't, and I don't particularly want to spend time with you, Jeff."

Eyebrows again.

"How did you know I'm named Jeff?"

"It's what I do, Jeff; now please leave me to my business."

Jeff gave a "your loss" shrug and retreated to the other end of the bar, his neck craning to see if there were any other targets.

The bartender, a slender blonde in her 30s, placed a bowl of mixed nuts in front of Charlaine.

"He tell you that you look like a movie star?"

"Yeah, Pam Grier."

"Oh my god. You're much prettier than she is."

"Thanks. She's also old enough to be my mother, but in the minds of guys of a certain age, she's still that woman from 'Jackie Brown' or if they're older, 'Foxy Brown'."

"Guess who he told me I looked like?"

"Laura Dern."

"How did you know that?"

"Lucky guess. Nothing against Laura, but you're better looking, and young enough to be her daughter."

"Thank you. I feel vindicated. Can I get you a bar menu?"

"No thanks, but maybe you can help me out. Did you see an Indian woman, late 20s, nicely dressed, come in?"

"I'm not supposed to give any information about comings or goings in here, but she could be in one of the private booths in the back. Give me your name and I can have Chaz, the maitre d', check discreetly."

"No, that's okay, she might be meeting someone so I'll wait."

Ten minutes later, Prisha emerged from the back room, accompanied by a gorgeous Black man who favored that baller they call The Greek Freak. Hmmm, this Prisha might not be what she seems, thought Charlaine, then thinking that the guy looked familiar. Not a Raven, and there's no professional basketball team in town, so she must have recognized him from somewhere else, maybe an issue of *Baltimore Magazine* listing the city's most eligible bachelors. Charlaine threw a $20 on the bar, waited about 10 seconds, and pushed through the door, sighting the couple talking briefly on the corner, then separating, Prisha striding quickly toward the parking garage and The Freak going in the opposite direction.

Charlaine paused for a moment, and decided to follow The Freak. She didn't know if it was the best professional move, but her curiosity got the best of her.

6

After separating from Prisha, Bernard checked his phone for emails or texts and finding none, tried to figure out what to do with the extra time he had before the gym opened. Prisha didn't want to stay for an early dinner and Bernard decided to leave with her. He was hungry but didn't want to stay in the booth without Prisha, and the bar and surrounding tables were becoming packed with happy hour celebrants and early evening diners. Thursday was a big night in Baltimore, with the heavy duty partiers not being able to wait for the weekend. Maybe he could get a taco and a coke from the El Rodeo truck that parked nearby Farley Recreation Center.

He took his time getting back to his car, parked four blocks away near a small one-story warehouse that was being renovated. There were a couple of knickknack shops along the square and he peered into the windows, thinking that his partner Kensey might like them. She loved these places when they traveled through small towns like Berlin and Havre De Grace. Although he appeared to be engaged in the window displays, his mind was on what Prisha had told him.

He thought about calling Roland but he needed time to frame questions so they wouldn't arouse suspicion. Prisha had assumed Roland was out of touch with what was going on at 3Make, but Bernard had a different perception. Roland had the spacey scientist demeanor down pat and could sit through an entire three-hour briefing without uttering a word, but then minutes, hours or days later would hit the engineering team with searing questions that belied his apparent stupor during the meeting.

But, it's possible that Roland didn't know anything about this nightshift work. If so, why was he being kept in the dark? Why would Bill Christenson, his hand-picked successor, keep a secret from his friend and mentor? And, perhaps most of all, why would the team working on the nightshift want to keep their research a secret if it was something potentially beneficial to the company?

Bernard didn't know everyone at 3Make; not since the company had grown to more than 150 people, most of them engineers. He tried to visit the company at least once a week and get introduced to the new hires, but sometimes they weren't there during his visits or he didn't get enough time with them.

Bernard prided himself on reading people, but 3Make was becoming increasingly diverse culturally and age-wise. He thought he knew most modern music, TV series, streaming sites, and personal technology developments, but he was constantly surprised at the new stuff that got under his net, and 3Make engineers were of practically every race and persuasion on earth. He was proud of that, but a bit uneasy about it as well. How do you gather all that diversity under one umbrella? Then he'd remember what his grandmother told him: "Bernard, you just listen, be nice and ask them about themselves. That's a universal language."

But nice only goes so far if you don't know what's going on. In those cases, nice can get your ass handed to you. He remembered what an older 3Make engineer who worked in quality control once told him. The saying was attributed to Ronald Reagan, but it was actually an old Russian proverb: "Trust but verify." The Russian term is better, since it rhymes: "Doveryai, no proveryai." In Bernard's mind, it meant that a responsible business person verifies everything before committing himself, even if a potential partner or hire has proven to be trustworthy in the past. Bernard believed that trust was not just built on reputation, but performance, time and time again.

So, okay, he'll start with Roland and begin to probe gently. He'll have to talk with Bill Christenson too because he can't have him keeping secrets from Prisha. Then finally, the 3Make chief operating officer, because he needs to have better intelligence about what's going on in his shop.

As he approached his car, Bernard saw a Lincoln Town Car parked in front of it. He'd been sad 10 years ago when they stopped making that car, as his uncle owned a fleet as part of his limo service. He remembered sitting with Tasha Morrow in the back of a stretch model, on their way to the senior prom, an ice bucket in the back chilling a bottle of Korbel Brut, and a Sherlock Holmes pipe stuffed with Sour Diesel.

Standing in front of the driver's side door of the Town Car was a short, red-headed woman in skintight black jeans and a cropped t-shirt, shivering and looking down at a piece of paper. She looked up at Bernard as he approached his 2013 Lexus ES 350.

"Sir, sir, could you help me with something?"

Bernard thought he wasn't old enough to be addressed as sir by an adult woman in her mid-20s, but it might have been the fact that she needed help that made her take that form of address.

"The name's Bernard. Can I help somehow?"

She looked at him like he'd just revealed the secret to a happy life.

"Oh, wow, yes, I hope. My dad loaned me his car and wrote down the pin on this piece of paper, but I left my glasses inside the car and I had a couple of drinks at happy hour. I'm embarrassed to say I can't read the combination. Could you open the door for me?"

Bernard smiled the smile that launched dozens of assignations. He didn't do that—the assignations, that is—anymore, but he could still turn on the smile effortlessly.

"You sure you want to ask a big Black man to do that? How do you know I won't open the door, take the keys from you, and drive away to my ghetto crib in your dad's prize Lincoln?"

The young woman chuckled and tilted her head in a way that Bernard had once heard described as "coquettish."

"No, I don't see Black or white. Besides, you have that bitchin' Lexus. Why would you want this old man's ride?"

Bernard walked up to within arm's length of the woman and stretched out his hand to receive the piece of paper. He looked at the numbers on the paper and began to input the first ones.

7

"Shit, dude, you knocked him out. You sure he isn't dead?"

Jackie's accomplice, Ashley, looked like a red-haired version of that woman from Jackie's favorite Nicolas Cage movie that he watched about three times a year. Holly something. And here they are staging a kidnapping, just like in the movie, except instead of a baby, they had a Black ex-basketball player and venture capital executive in the trunk.

Ashley was a former actress. She'd had a leading role in the Community College of Baltimore's production of *The Fantasticks*, and had done a TV spot for the duckpin lanes on Eastern Avenue. That was five years ago. These days she was trying to hold down a nightshift at a Royal Farms store while managing a rapidly growing coke habit, which was how she was being paid for her latest role as a despondent young woman trying to figure out the five-number pin for her daddy's car door. She didn't know that there would be violence involved, but she didn't seem too disturbed by it, cruising down Light Street toward Hanover with an eight-ball burning a hole in the pocket of her jeans.

Jackie wondered how Ashley could fit anything in that pocket or even how she could sit in those jeans without ripping them at their straining seams. But, he was strangely calm and happy. Must have been that joint Buck had given him, letting him know that it was strategic; that it would "mellow out his nervous ass."

Jackie had been concerned. Why wouldn't he be? Kidnapping a big, athletic Black man. Jackie didn't use the "n" word. He'd grown up and played football with all kinds of guys and didn't think there were any inherent differences. Inherent. Nice. He'd been trying to stretch his vocabulary recently, reading the *Sun* daily and checking out books from the library. The classics: Stephen King. James Patterson. Lee Child. He'd love a gig at the library, among all those books, talking with other people who read. Erudite people. Yeah, erudite. Nice one, Jackie!

He didn't really know Ashley, having been introduced to her the night before by Buck, who'd met her while he was smoking a blunt in Poe Park. Buck boasted about him picking up this hot chick, but there was no evidence of an amorous attachment that Jackie could see, other than their mutual attraction to weed and blow. Jackie was fine with the weed, but the blow was out of bounds for him. He was naturally uptight, and coke would have been like giving a 20-ounce bottle of Jolt Cola to a toddler.

The plan could have gone wrong in a lot of ways. Jackie could have lost Jamal on the way from his office to Canton. He could have been unable to find a parking place near Jamal's car and would have had to improvise another scenario or wait a day or two for another opportunity. He could have easily messed up the blow to the head, although he had rehearsed it using a pressure pad applied to the head of a boxing dummy raised at the same height as Jamal's head.

Jackie had been worried about Ashley getting ripped and messing up the job, but she was a true pro, reacting only after she saw the Black dude go down after Jackie's blow to the temple with the butt of his revolver. Jackie was shaken by this as well. The dude fell like Joe Frazier after that overhead punch by Foreman in their first fight. *Down goes Frazier, down goes Frazier* thought Jackie, as the guy crumpled to the pavement.

Jackie had his apprehensions about the plan from the beginning, as Buck had never done something so big. His bread and butter was two-bit stuff, like shoplifting, auto theft, and small-time dealing. Buck wanted to use chloroform on Jamal, telling Jackie that it's simple: "Just like in the movies. Come up behind him, put a handkerchief soaked with the stuff over his nose, and it's done. Use that country-boy muscle to lift him into the trunk and away you go."

But Jackie didn't want to take Buck's word for anything. He knew about all the bogus things that went down flawlessly in movies, but were not that easy in real life. Sure enough, when he went online and researched it, he found out that a person would have to breathe in a lot of chloroform over a few minutes to go down, and even then you wouldn't know for how long or how toxic it would be. After researching other knockout solutions, he thought the gun butt was the best plan, although that had its problems too, worst of which were the guy not getting knocked out and attacking like a rabid bull or just dying on the spot. Fortunately, Bernard Jamal did neither. He fell immediately and stayed knocked out as Jackie wrestled him into the trunk of the car.

It all went down flawlessly, except for the witness.

8

Charlaine watched from behind a parked car half a block up the street as the Black dude who looked like The Greek Freak approached his car. Nice ride if you didn't mind a boring Lexus. He paused at the driver's side door and then said something to a compact redhead in front of the driver's door of a Lincoln Town Car. Shit, that's a classic that brings back memories. Charlaine fucked Ronnie McAndrews, that fine guard from Edmondson, in the back seat of his father's Town Car. All was okay until Ronnie told all of his teammates, who turned around and broadcast it throughout West Baltimore. Ronnie tried to keep hitting on her after that, but Charlaine froze out his snitching ass. Discretion was hard to find in Charlaine's world, especially among men.

Charlaine was pretending to open a car door when out of the corner of her eye she saw a big bear-like motherfucker come from behind the other side of the Town Car and knock the Freak out with the butt of his gun. She was briefly impressed, thinking she had never seen it done so cleanly—a rap on the temple and down he went. She started to run toward the Town Car when the girl saw her and quietly nudged the big guy. The big guy pointed the revolver at Charlaine, who backed off with her hands in the air.

"Stay cool and keep your mouth shut," hissed the big guy, handing the gun to the girl and commanding her to cover him while he stuffed the Freak into the trunk. The gun was a medium-sized model, a .357 by the looks of it. It was huge in the girl's hand, but she held it steady, offering a "turn around sister and face the other way" in a calm, clear voice. Charlaine didn't know what was going down and obeyed the girl, thinking *Just wait until I get your little Lucy-looking ass one on one and we'll see how confident you are.*

9

It could have been worse. The ride was smooth and Bernard could stretch his legs out if he laid down diagonally. He could sleep in there if he had a blanket and his mind wasn't firing like an AR15.

Something above his ear was pulsing like a metronome, each beat sending a rivulet of pain through his head. His hands were bound behind him, plastic digging into his wrists. His wallet was gone from his back pocket and when he rolled onto his stomach he couldn't feel the lump of his cellphone in his left pocket. He turned on his side and felt along the wall of the trunk until he came upon a compartment. He was able to open the flap with his fingers and felt the jack and the plastic bag that holds the tire iron. He could have untied the string securing the bag, but then what good would it do to have a tire iron when his wrists were bound behind his back?

Bernard could hear AC/DC playing in the car. "Highway to Hell" never sounded so threatening. *Who are these people and why him?* He tried to piece together what happened and could only remember the meeting with Prisha and the name Spencer Ohtari. Why would he be thinking of Ohtari? He barely knew him before he was ousted from Sintology. The car slowed to a stop, which got Bernard's attention. The music didn't stop and he didn't hear any doors close, so it was probably just a red light or stop sign, but it raised an alarm in Bernard's mind. They could reach their destination at any moment and he had to have a plan.

That's when he thought about the length of his legs and basic leverage. The trunk was deep, allowing Bernard to lay on his back with his legs coiled for a kick. If he could inch his way to the outer edge of the trunk, he might be able to rise up on his forearms and kick one of these motherfuckers in the balls. He just hoped there weren't two of them and there were no guns involved. The surprise factor was the only thing on his side.

10

Ashley opened the baggy, her hands shaking in anticipation. She scooped up a little powder on the tip of the long fingernail of her baby finger and snorted it in her left nostril, repeating the process with her right nostril. She pulled up her chin and rested the back of her head on the headrest, her red lashes falling gently on her cheeks. She looked serene to Jackie.

He turned down the AC/DC, looked over at her and smiled involuntarily. She looked over at him at the same time.

"Hey, why'd you turn down the jams?"

"I just wanted to let you know that you did a great job back there. Cool as a cucumber. Like you've been there before."

"How do you know I haven't been?"

"You look so innocent. I mean, not with the gun in your hand or snorting that shit, but before…"

"Yeah, it's part of my MO. Lookin' like Little Red Riding Hood, while I'm all wolfish and shit inside. It's gotten me some things. And, I'm an actor, remember? I can improv like nobody's business. My acting teacher told me that I'm one of the best he's ever seen. Like Elaine May, he said. I'd never heard of her so I YouTubed her. She did a bunch of shit with a guy in a bad wig."

"Mike Nichols, yeah."

"How did you know? You must be a lot older than you look."

"Nah. I study entertainers, and I just read the Mike Nichols biography."

"Were they married?"

"Nah. Just lifelong friends."

"Oh, that's sweet."

"Why do you say that?"

"Because sex ruins everything, especially friendship."

They were crossing the Patapsco River on the Hanover Street Bridge, now called the Vietnam Veterans Memorial Bridge. The surface was lumpy with heaved asphalt and even the heavy Town Car was bumping up and down. Nice memorial for the Vietnam vets, thought Jackie. Typical after-the-fact shit. His uncle died over there and he's memorialized by a shitty bridge.

Jackie looked over as Ashley tried to load another hit onto her nail, finally giving up in frustration. They'd be at Buck's place soon and she would take off to McSweeny's bar before Buck could corner her. She'd done her work and wasn't going to share her pay with Buck, who could suck up an eight-ball like a Hoover.

"You're awfully young to be so cynical," said Jackie. "Don't you think there is a chance for love in your life?"

"Sure, plenty of chances, just as long as it doesn't involve sex."

Glad we got that out of the way, thought Jackie, although it had never been in the way to begin with.

11

Bernard felt the car turn right into a gravel road or driveway and slow to a stop. He scooched to the outer edge of the trunk, pulling his legs as far back as possible and tensing his forearms for the outward spring. He was strangely calm, as if he was standing at the free throw line for the first of two shots. Bernard was an 82% free throw shooter in college, so he knew how to calm himself down while under the forces of adrenaline.

The trunk popped and Bernard had a glimpse of massive thighs encased in denim. He had planned to go for the balls, but quickly recalibrated to the left knee. If he missed the balls, he was a dead man, but he could arc up and come down with both feet on the guy's left knee. Guys that big almost always have bad knees, carrying around all that excess poundage.

When the lid of the trunk reached its peak, Bernard leaped. The guy had stepped back from the trunk and Bernard fell short of his mark, his feet hitting just below the guy's left knee. Fortunately for Bernard, the left knee was Jackie's worst one, and even though the hit was below the knee, it sent the giant staggering backwards and falling on his ass. Bernard fell too, twisting his ankle as he rolled to the side of the big man. He saw a flash of metal in the guy's right hand and stomped on his wrist. The guy yelped in pain, but held onto the gun. Bernard looked up and saw a redhead sprinting across the street and into an intersecting alley. Then he heard the screen door of the adjoining house slam and saw a man at the bottom of the steps flashing some steel in his left hand.

Bernard took off across the street to what looked like an abandoned warehouse, weaving in and out so as not to present a linear target. He must have learned something from all those cop shows he used to watch, because the bullets were flying to the left and right or behind him. Maybe the guy was just a shitty shot.

Bernard hadn't planned on how hard it is to run with your hands behind you. His ankle was swelling and shot his leg with pain each time his left foot landed on the concrete, but he clambered on, ducking behind a brick wall and leaning forward in the cold air. He looked behind him and couldn't see the guy with the gun; either he hadn't pursued him or was not in the kind of condition to run very far or fast. Still, no time to stop or rest. Keep moving, like a rat down an alley. He went through the warehouse, stopping every ten yards to hide behind a pole in case the gunman entered the building. He finally came out the other side, where he saw a residential street of row houses to his left and more industrial ruins to his right, with a glimpse of water on the horizon. He had a naturally good sense of direction, and when he was in the trunk he thought they were heading south, then perhaps a bit west. He'd been in the car for about 20 minutes or so by his estimate, which could be off since he didn't know how long he'd been unconscious. He figured he was in the south part of the city, or maybe just over the city line in Baltimore County.

He thought of turning left and going through the residential area, knocking on a door and seeing if he could explain his predicament. But, who would he get coming to the door? He tried to tell by the parked cars whether the neighborhood was Black or white, but it was hard to tell, and there was nobody on the street. It was a poor neighborhood, which in a racially divided city like Baltimore would likely mean it was a Black area. But what if he was wrong? If he knocked on a door and a white man answered, he could be in trouble. Who would believe a handcuffed Black man was the victim and not a suspect running from the cops?

Just then he heard voices, white ones, one guy yelling at another. He ran to the back of the row house on the corner, where he saw a tarp covering what looked like a row boat atop a pair of sawhorses. He turned his back to the boat, fell to his knees, and lifted the tarp with his hand-cuffed fingers. Falling face first to the ground, he crawled under the boat, hoping that the pair of guys with guns hadn't seen him. He stuck his head out from the lip of the rowboat and brushed away the tarp to get a glimpse of the two men. The big one was limping, heavily favoring the right knee. He was obviously in pain, both physically and mentally, as the other guy kept yelling at him. Bernard could now see why the other guy couldn't pursue him; he was stocky, but had a gut spilling over his pants. Football players gone to seed, Bernard thought. He just hoped they wouldn't comb through the backyards looking for potential hiding places.

Luckily for Bernard, they headed down the street, looking into the front windows of the row houses, many still covered in the distinctive Baltimore formstone overtop the brick exterior. That was a sign it was an old neighborhood, one that was not under gentrification, as most people refurbishing those types of homes removed the formstone to expose the original brick, re-pointing the concrete and sometimes whitewashing the surface.

Bernard heard a loud banging on the screen door of the house next door to the one in which he was hiding in the backyard. He strained to listen. The occupant had come out on the front stoop to talk to the two guys pursuing Bernard. Their voices carried in the chilly night air and Bernard could hear snippets of the conversation. The two would-be kidnappers were struggling to remain calm. He could hear the occupant of the house, who sounded to Bernard like an old Black man, keep repeating something that sounded like "Nope, didn't see nothin'" over and over again as the two white guys pressed him and became increasingly agitated. They finally gave up and went on to the next house.

Bernard stayed under the row boat and the tarp for what he estimated to be an hour. Given the condition of his two assailants, he figured that they couldn't keep up the chase on foot too much longer than that. He crawled out from under the boat and tarp and decided to take a chance. He got up slowly, tested his sore ankle and wobbled up the alley to the neighbor's house. When he got to the front he peered around the corner and looked up and down the block. Seeing no one on the street he walked up the first step and suddenly felt dizzy, falling flat on his stomach and banging his head on the screen door.

12

Charlaine walked the four blocks to the parking garage quickly, wanting to run but not chancing a twisted ankle on the heels she was wearing to fit in with the Formosa clientele.

She thought again about calling Tony, but dismissed it a second time. She trusted him, but the sequence of events had set her head afire with confusion. Who was The Freak and why was he meeting with Prisha? Did she set him up? If so, how did she know where he'd park? Was Prisha in league with the big white dude and little Lucy? And if so, whatever for? She was pulling down a mill a year or so not counting ownership options. She was married to a guy who had an equally good job and they had a son at St. Paul's in Brooklandville. She didn't need money, so maybe something else was driving this, whatever this is.

Charlaine hated incomplete information more than anything. That's what both drove her crazy and motivated her to get at the truth, however hazy it might be. She'd talk to Joy. Joy would get her straight. Joy was an art instructor at The Park School and made a good living with her own art, collages depicting everyday life in old Baltimore neighborhoods and small towns in the Maryland countryside. People tend to stereotype artists as scatterbrains, always thinking in the abstract, displacing reality with dreamy tangents or angry dismissals. But Joy was always in the moment with Charlaine, calming her when she needed it and supporting her when she felt like she was on shaky ground. Like she was now.

Charlaine had promised Tony that she wouldn't talk about the case to anyone, not even Joy, but what she'd just witnessed changed the deal. Tony had concealed something important from her, and boss or no, she'd call him on it. But first, home to discuss it with Joy, her rock. She got to the car, took off the heels and threw them in the backseat, dug the phone from her bag, and hit "Joy."

"Yes, my dear?"

"I have to speak with you darling. Are you home?"

"You sound like Harried Charlaine, whom I love, but not as much as Charming Charlaine."

"Are you home?"

"Just got here and I have crab cakes, coleslaw and a Donna's Salad, the one with Buffalo chicken and blue cheese dressing, from Koco's. I thought I'd surprise you, but it sounds like you need something to look forward to."

"Yes I do. But more than that I need your brain and sanity. There's a nice Oregon Pinot Gris in the hutch. Could you put that on ice for us?"

"Brain and sanity are all yours, Precious, and I'll put the Pinot in the fridge to chill. Where are you and when will you get here?"

"Leaving Canton and if all goes well traffic-wise, be there in about a half hour."

Traffic wasn't too bad and 35 minutes later Charlaine pulled into the driveway and onto the parking pad at the back of the house. They had what the realtor called a two-car garage, but it could only fit two cars if they were those so-called Smart Cars, which Charlaine didn't think were too clever at all. They'd decided after moving in that the garage would be Joy's studio, a place to get away without leaving their property.

The house was a two-story, four-bedroom, three-bath brick number built in the mid-30s, with hardwood floors in the public areas, tile in the bathrooms, and carpeting in the bedrooms. Lots of nice touches that the realtor called "features" when they first looked at the place three years ago. Joy and Charlaine used the master bedroom and bath, kitted out one of the bedrooms as a guestroom, turned one into Charlaine's office, and used the other to store assorted stuff, which was multiplying at an alarming rate. The basement was finished and included an exercise area and a laundry room.

They didn't need all the space, but they'd fallen in love with the house: the wide-plank, dark brown floors; the generous crown molding; the arched front door with the steep ceiling entryway; the small, but well-appointed kitchen with granite counters and stainless-steel appliances; the 12-panel windows that opened with a pulley; the hefty hearth of the fireplace. The lot was narrow, but went back about 60 yards. Joy wanted a dog that could run around back there, but Charlaine said she wasn't ready yet for that kind of commitment.

Charlaine was walking toward the back porch when Joy appeared holding a cocktail glass and wearing a smile. Despite everything, Charlaine smiled back. She always did. All it took was looking at Joy, a gorgeous slice of pure Baltimorious beauty: The alabaster skin, the thick black hair, the tight frame, the classic face always alight with wonder.

"That's a sight for some really sore eyes."

Joy laughed and those hazel eyes twinkled.

"Me or the martini?"

"You, darling. The martini I can make, but I couldn't make you in my wildest dreams."

"Flattery will get you everywhere, provided you want to go there."

"I want to go there alright, but I've got some business to discuss for now."

Joy handed off the martini to Charlaine and opened the back door for her. Charlaine went inside, plopped down on the distressed leather couch, and put the drink on an end table. Joy sat across from her on a heavily padded easy chair.

"So, what's the story? Haven't seen you this serious since J.K. Dobbins went down with that ACL."

"This beats that by a mile. You ever witness an abduction?"

Charlaine took a deep draw of martini and spilled the story, leaving out no details and stopping herself from rushing too quickly to the finish. When it was over, Joy sat with her mouth agape, a look that was new to both of them.

"Why didn't you call the cops?"

Charlaine expected that question. Joy had grown up in Dulaney Valley and that's what people did when they saw trouble, no questions asked. For Charlaine, growing up in West Baltimore, it was more complicated, with the police rarely being an option. It annoyed her that Joy didn't know this by now, but she tried to hide her frustration.

"I was on a case and how am I supposed to explain what I was doing there following this guy when my car was in a parking garage four blocks in the opposite direction? Then there's Tony and the case itself. I'm supposed to be tracking the Indian woman, Prisha, not The Freak."

"Why do you call him The Freak?"

"You know, The Greek Freak? Two-time NBA MVP? Antetokounmpo?" Charlaine was proud of pronouncing his name correctly; she had practiced it in the car before venturing to say it to Joy out loud. She figured a guy that good should get the respect of his name being pronounced properly.

"Oooo, now I know who you mean. Sexy, sexy man."

"Yeah, agreed. But this BMore version was knocked out, thrown into a trunk, and wheeled away in front of my eyes." Charlaine knew Joy's next question before she asked it.

"So, why not go to Tony?"

"I'm trying to trust Tony on this, baby, but it's not adding up. I mean, I follow this woman into a bar, she meets with a man, and the moment she leaves, the man gets knocked out and thrown into a trunk. There seems to be cause and effect."

"But you don't know that. It's speculation. You don't know what you don't know. How long have you worked for Tony? Six years? Why would he get you involved in something like this?"

"Exactly my thought. Why? But Tony likes his money."

"Who doesn't? But if I'm Tony I'm not going to jeopardize my best employee and the future of my business. What's he, mid 50s? He's not ready to retire, is he? Unless this is some kind of huge payoff. And if he doesn't want you to discover something, why put you on the case instead of Kepler?"

Andy Kepler was an older guy that Tony kept in the agency as a favor to a former PI with whom he'd apprenticed. He might have been competent at one time, but Charlaine couldn't imagine it; the guy she's known for the last six years couldn't track a dog through a house if the pooch was leaving muddy paw prints.

Charlaine took another hit of the martini and leaned back on the sofa. She hadn't realized that she was sitting on the edge of the sofa with her foot tapping the wooden floor. Joy got off her chair and kneeled in front of her, wrapping her hands around Charlaine's.

"Call Tony, Charlaine. Be straight with him. Tell him you can't be left out of the loop. You won't work that way. You know there are other agencies that would love to have you onboard if it comes to that. Don't threaten, but be firm about it. You know the Force is with you."

Joy loved that Star Wars shit, whereas Charlaine didn't give a good fuck about it. Her Force was Joy, and she was with her, always, whether physically present or not. Charlaine decided to take a shower, call Tony, then tuck into those crab cakes.

13

Joe Monroe sat back on his BarcaLounger, a freshly opened bottle of Heineken at his side, getting ready for the tipoff of the Wizards' playoff game. He didn't like the Wizards that much, since in his mind Washington had stolen the team from Baltimore and changed the name from the Bullets in an early fit of political correctness. He came from the era where you could get a student ticket for $2.75 and sit in the upper deck of the Baltimore Civic Center, still not far from the court, a lot closer than in these huge arenas they build these days.

Joe thought kids these days didn't know about NBA history further back than Kobe, much less about the high-wire act of the Bullets' Gus Johnson, who broke a backboard in Milwaukee that rained glass on the head of the rookie Lew Alcindor; or the original Magic, Earl Monroe, the whirling dervish who could barely dunk a basketball but would dominate a game, causing nightmares for the likes of his future teammate Walt Frazier; and, of course, that first-round draft pick out of Louisville, Wes Unseld, the rebounding machine with the fastest, most accurate outlet pass known to man.

He'd been in the same house for 40 years, all of them while married to Dinah before pancreatic cancer took her away five years ago. Their son John had joined the Army 20 years ago and now was on the verge of retiring. Joe found it hard to believe that he had a son who was retiring, but he was 73, with Dinah, his parents, brothers and sisters, aunts and uncles, and all but a couple of cousins gone. Most of the guys he worked with on road crews throughout the city were gone too. Black men in Baltimore City didn't have the best life spans, especially if they worked hard labor jobs all their lives.

Joe lived a pretty good life. His only vices, if you wanted to call them that, were the Heinekens, the occasional pop of Hennessy, and a weekly lottery ticket. He would have been lonely except for the Brooklyn branch of the Enoch Pratt Free Library, where he fed his insatiable appetite for crime novels. He loved the classics—Cain, Hammett, Chandler, Christie, MacDonald, Leonard—and the Black writers, especially Walter Mosley, who had 60 novels to his name, and those youngsters, Attica Locke, S.A. Cosby, Rachel Howzell Hall. He loved reading novels set in Baltimore, like those from Robert Ward and Laura Lippman, the ex-*Sun* reporter. Venture farther south into DC and there was George Pelecanos, who wrote better about the streets and basketball courts of the inner city than anyone.

Joe probably had enough in savings to move to the suburbs like some of his friends, but he was okay in Curtis Bay, despite the increase in crime and lack of neighborhood camaraderie. Joe hadn't experienced much worse than attempted break-ins, but he was aware of his neighborhood's demographics. The south part of Curtis Bay where he lived was the worst section of the neighborhood, with an overall crime rate 49 percent higher than the city as a whole, and five times the state of Maryland's rate. Joe was certain that most blamed the increasing crime on a greater influx of Black people. Curtis Bay was now about half white and half Black. When he first moved into the area with Dinah, it was overwhelmingly white.

Like most of Baltimore City, there were old white people wishing Curtis Bay would have stayed the same as it was when they were growing up. Joe had even found a group on Facebook dedicated to the old Curtis Bay. The group is all white and full of lament for the way things were and what could've or should've been done to save the neighborhood. But none of them live there anymore or have done anything to help the neighborhood in which they grew up.

The neighbors might not have sent around a welcome wagon when Joe and Dinah first moved into their 1,200-square-foot row house, but they left them alone. Joe was a hard worker and kept to himself, and Dinah was a teacher at Curtis Bay Middle School, so they were tolerated as long as they didn't play loud music or invite large numbers of Black friends to parties at their house. By the time their son John entered Southern High, playing football and basketball, he had friends of all races throughout the neighborhood.

In the last few years, gangs—the white Dead Man Inc., the Black Crips, and the MS-13 Hispanic crew—had set their sights on different territories in the neighborhood. Joe didn't feel endangered, but just walking the streets, sitting on the stoop, or watching TV in your living room across from a street-front window could be risky.

Those two white boys banging on his door and trying to intimidate him didn't particularly bother him, except they were looking for a Black man and seemed to insinuate that Joe was hiding something. Sure as shit he would have been, especially given their story of a guy who skipped bail and escaped from their custody. Joe knew that bounty hunters didn't look like choir boys—what was the name of that long-haired, pumped-up white guy and his big tittied wife who was on TV all the time about 10 years ago?—but these guys looked like they couldn't wrangle a dead snake. And, shit, trying to intimidate him? They were big, but Joe always felt the harder they come, the harder they fall, and he'd made a few of them fall in his younger years.

Joe was tossing an empty Heineken into the recycling bin when something banged against the bottom of the front screen door. *Shit, what now*, he thought. If it's those white boys he might be inclined to call the police, although that was usually his last resort.

He went to the window beside the front door and saw a tall Black man splayed across the stoop, his hands shackled behind his back with those zip ties they use nowadays. His clothes looked expensive to Joe, who used to be able to clean up nicely for a night of disco at Odell's on St. Paul Street, but in the last decade mostly dressed in track suits except for funerals and the rare wedding.

Joe tried to open the front screen door but the man was wedged in close enough that he couldn't squeeze by. He went out the back door, opened the gate to the alley and circled around to the front, looking around him to see if anyone was watching. He eased the man down to the second step, enough to open the screen door, and shoved the front door open with his foot. He grabbed the big man underneath his armpits and dragged him into the living room, being careful not to hit his head, which already had a lump on it the size of the miniature crab cakes Dinah used to make for po'boy subs.

Joe got the guy inside the door and again peeked left and right to see if anyone was watching before closing it. He dragged the big man beside the small sofa and boosted him up on it, resting his head on a pillow at the foot of one armrest and extending his legs beyond the far armrest. The guy looked faintly familiar to Joe, like a ballplayer, maybe a local guy from high school or college. Joe wasn't good with gauging age, but placed him roughly in his late 20s or early 30s, in good shape with a barrel chest tapering to a slim waist. *How did he fall in with those raggedy ass white boys?*

Joe thought again about calling the cops, but hesitated. The guy didn't look like anybody's idea of a criminal, but in Joe's experience most cops arrested first and asked questions later. The guy didn't have a phone on him and his wallet was gone, so Joe had no way of identifying him. For now, Joe thought he could make the guy comfortable and see if he could revive him. He went into the kitchen and took some ice cubes from the freezer, using Dinah's wooden rolling pin to crush them on two dish towels and tying the towels into pouches. He placed one of the pouches under the lump that bulged out red and angry from the man's temple. He took off the big man's shoes and placed the other pouch on his swollen ankle. *Must have been that big-ass limping white guy, the one who looked like an old-timey pro wrassler, that hit the guy in the temple. The other guy couldn't stretch the belly of his enough to reach up to the man's temple. They must have taken him by surprise or else held a gun on him to put the zip ties on his wrists behind his back.*

Joe left the guy on the couch and went out the back door to his small storage shed, unlocking the heavy combination lock and getting his garden shears. He rolled the guy, who he was now calling Doctor J, on his side and gnawed away at the ties, eventually getting to the point where he could snip them loose. He set them on the coffee table, thinking that they could be a visual reminder to the Doctor when he gained consciousness, which Joe wished would happen soon. He wondered what the Doctor's assailants were doing, still looking for the escapee or giving up for the night and turning themselves to the comfort of weed and whiskey.

14

Tony Mancuso was at the top of the fold-out bleacher seats watching his 13-year-old son struggle to bring the ball past half court against this skinny Black kid with fast feet and hands. Tony never wanted his son to play basketball. He was built like Tony growing up—chunky, with a thick torso and an ass like a Tonka toy truck. Could be a catcher, a hockey goalie, maybe a lacrosse defenseman, although the last one would be a stretch. Anything but the point guard he aspired to be after seeing that kid from the Charlotte Hornets. One of the Ball kids. Father's a real ass, but the kids seem to be alright. JaMale? Lamar? LeMarcus? No, LaMelo. That's it. How could Tony forget; his kid wore the jersey just about every day and reported on the guy's stats from the previous night every morning at breakfast.

Tony's son might have liked LaMelo because he has a similar name. His son is named Carmelo, but not after Carmelo Anthony, the NBA player from Baltimore. Carmelo Mancuso is named for a driver who chauffeured Tony and his wife Lidia around the Amalfi Coast, leading to the night in Sorrento when they thought their son was conceived. Or it could have been the next night in Positano.

The young Carmelo was trying to dribble with his left hand when the skinny kid stripped him of the ball and dribbled in for an easy layup. Carmelo complained to the ref that he was hacked, but Tony thought it was a clean swipe, no different from the kid's previous four steals in the first half.

Tony was daydreaming about another night in Rome when Lidia gave him a full body rubdown when his phone rang. He saw it was Charlaine and answered quietly, walking quickly down the bleachers toward the door.

"What's up Goddess?"

Tony had these nicknames. He had read a book by Charlamagne tha God that purported to be a guide to the hood and quoted from it all the time. He first started calling Charlaine "Charlaine tha Goddess" and then shortened it to "Tha Goddess" and eventually just "Goddess." Charlaine almost considered herself fortunate. Tony called Jose Rodiguez "No Way," as in "No Way Jose" and he dubbed Kleper "Colony." The agency's long-time receptionist, a 70-year-old, blue-haired woman named Barbara, became "Barbie" and then just "Doll."

"Can you talk, Tony?"

"My wife says I can't, but I do alright with other people. What can I do you for?"

Charlaine had practiced telling her story with Joy, who urged her to cut out extraneous and emotional stuff—*just the facts, Jack*. When she got to the end she gave her first editorial comment: "I don't appreciate being in the dark, Tony."

For once, Tony didn't have a joke. Charlaine was sure he had a line about being left in the dark, like that one he told about the baseball player, Tug something, who said he was terrified the first time he had sex: "It was dark and I was alone."

"I didn't want to burden you with a bunch of extrastraineous info, Goddess. Did you call the cops?"

"You know me better than that Tone."

"It's a bizarro incident, for certain, but I can't see how it could be related to the case."

"Bizarre is putting it mildly. Let's cut to the chase: Why am I following this Prisha woman?"

"Okay, I'll tell you, but you have to be discretionary about it."

"Discretionary is my middle name."

"Hmmm, didn't know that. I thought it was Aliya or something like that. Anyway, our client, whom I can't name, said Prisha is suspected of embezzlement or some other kind of funny business and we're trying to find out what's happening. I've got Jacey doing the computer stuff and you're the feet on the ground."

"I could have been the feet *in* the ground if little Lucy had fired that pistol, so you need to come up with some more details about who's employing us and why. I mean, do you really think Prisha is the type?"

"When it comes to money, there ain't a type, Goddess. The mean green is an equal opportunity employer."

"But she seems to have no need. What's her motive?"

"Motive, schmotive. We're like chiropractors, Godful One; we don't care about the cause, only getting rid of the pain."

"I care. A lot. And if you want me on this, you better care too. Information, Tone, information, or my fine ass is out of here."

"Okay, okay. Sheesh. You don't need to threaten disemployment."

"I don't threaten, Tony. I lay down the law."

"Got you Goddess. I'll get to the bottom of this. And if we find that Freak guy maybe we can ask him to teach Carmelo how to go left with his dribble."

"Yeah, and I'm going to star in Spike Lee's next joint. Call me when you find out more about our client, Tony. Meanwhile, I'm going to find out what happened to Baltimore's Antetokounmpo."

"Wow, impressive. I think you're ready for ESPN."

Tony hung up, shaking his head but thinking that Charlaine had a right to be upset. He had been uneasy about accepting payment without knowing the source and exactly what they wanted. But, the money was good and where was the harm? Well, he guessed he was seeing the harm. But these are nerds, not the kind of people who could knock out a Black man the size of Anteto-whatever. What's the connection?

Tony didn't want to admit it to Charlaine, but he was also uneasy about the subject of the investigation. Prisha seemed unimpeachably honest. And even though he told Charlaine that motive didn't matter, he too was bothered by the lack of it. But, he'd seen less likely candidates in the past. Engineers giving out proprietary information to competitors for a mere slither of their annual salaries. A CFO skimming pension funds to buy her kids a swimming pool. Construction companies skimping on the concrete mix to earn an extra five percent on a state-funded project. A local politico taking money passed to him in the john of a third-class strip joint. A cub scout leader dipping his hand into the till for a couple hundred bucks.

Who knows what motivates these people? It goes beyond money in Tony's mind, or why would people with more money than God commit these kinds of crimes? They all have their reasons, and if caught some reveal it. They felt overworked, underappreciated, left out of the company largesse. They wanted to screw the ownership where it hurts. Or, they just wanted to prove that they're smarter than anybody else: ego running amok.

People tend to think embezzlement, kickbacks and skimming are crimes in which the perps will get caught and eventually prosecuted. But Tony knew the reality was quite different. In an embezzlement case, the burden of proof is on the prosecutor, who has to prove beyond a reasonable doubt that the defendant had a specific intent to defraud the victim of property. Tony read that many don't get caught and 40 percent of the ones who do get caught aren't prosecuted.

The first red flag about Prisha was the background check done by Jacey Creed, his computer expert. It showed nothing. Not a parking ticket. Not a financial blemish. Prisha and her husband were rich, but spent in keeping with their salaries and investments. The investments were well balanced and on the conservative side, and there were no luxury purchases that would have raised alarms: No villa on Lake Como, no 100-foot yacht, no secret stash of vintage cars, art or jewelry. Tony had never seen a suspect without blemishes, but he appeared to have one now in Prisha.

Jacey was working on finding out who the client might be from their text messages and email, but they were good. Very good. Like Russian hacker good. That made Tony nervous. These were professionals and for all Tony knew they could be hacking his agency's computers and phones, although Jacey said no way. Jacey has never been mistaken before, but even Mike Tyson met his match eventually, and Tony wondered if he should get somebody else on the case.

But he could just be paranoid. That was part of his job description, of course. You can't do what he and his investigators do without being hyper-suspicious. Suspicious to a fault, Tony always said. Don't even trust your mama. But that's a tough way to live. Tony tries to separate work from home life, but it bleeds through. A couple of weeks ago, Tony interrogated Lidia about the butcher throwing in an extra chop. Sure he was joking, but Lidia detected an edge. A few days later, he grilled Carmelo about customized Adidas sneakers he said he bought from a classmate for $50. Tony researched the sneakers and found they can sell for $200 or more, depending on the condition. He called the kid's parents and they confirmed the sale. Tony apologized to Carmelo, but he still hasn't gotten back to normal terms with his son.

Tony had begun to think that suspicion was wearing him out, stripping his essential humanity. Lidia called him out again last week after a dinner party when Tony told her everything potentially wrong with every person in the room. "What happened to simple trust, Tony," she asked. Tony told her it went the way of the dodo bird, but lately he's woken up in the middle of the night in a cold sweat. How much is too much? Why can't he turn it off at the end of the work day? But that's just it; there's no end of the work day. Tony always told potential hires that if they wanted a 9 to 5 job to run, don't walk, to the nearest exit.

But all this pondering of the future and how he can change his behavior wasn't doing a bit of good at the moment. Tony knew what he had to do and should have done from the beginning: Get to the bottom of who hired him and the real reason why. And if Jacey couldn't find that out via the computer, he had to go old-school. Because as much as technology can be a huge tool in the search for the truth, nothing worked like getting directly into people's heads and making them uncomfortable. He knew that Charlaine would work like a relentless house fly on finding the Freak, and he'd have to do the same for the phantom client.

But first, he'd have to sit through the second half of Carmelo being Carmelo.

15

Four miles away from the scene of Carmelo's humiliation, eight guys were finishing up their pick-up games at the Farley Recreation Center. Four-on-four games, each basket counting for one point, first to get to 11, but you have to win by two baskets. They'd been doing this for three years now, with John Summers and his friend Bernard Jamal handling the arrangements. The players were anywhere from 25 to 30-something. Most had played high school ball and a couple had played college hoops for small schools. The court was three-quarters length, which worked just fine for once-a-week guys.

They came from different backgrounds. Black, white, Hispanic, Asian. IT guys. An insurance salesman. A guy who leased hospital beds. A history teacher. A couple of guys who worked for county road crews. Summers and Jamal were considered the Alphas, having played varsity at UWB; Summers a slender 6' 3" guard and Jamal a muscular 6' 6" forward who liked nothing better than banging inside, but could also do some damage from 18-20 foot range.

They naturally broke up into two teams by an established protocol. When Summers and Jamal first rented the gym, it was just guys that they knew and hung with. But by the second year, that group began to thin out due to the usual cause: responsibilities at home or work. One night when they were exhausting themselves playing whole court three-on-three, five guys walked into the gym looking like an advertisement for male diversity:

A 6' 7" gawky white guy, a lithesome 5'8" Black guy, a chubby 6' 2" Asian guy a bit younger than the rest, and a pair of 6' Hispanic twins whose names nobody figured out.

The new guys would play and then go home, to where, Summers and Jamal never knew. They didn't do much talking between games. They were there to play basketball. It was a refuge for like-minded guys who no longer had athletic dreams but still wanted to keep a hand in the game they loved. They would disagree about fouls, which they called themselves, but rarely were voices raised and there was no untoward physical contact. It was a kind of utopia for men who still wanted to compete, but didn't want it to be a life-or-death matter. It was a rare thing to be able to assemble this kind of group, because most men never give up their desire to reduce the competition to rubble.

Tonight the players quit earlier than usual, as there were only eight of them and no substitutes. The biggest absence was Bernard, who had not missed a Thursday night game in the years they'd rented the gym. He was the catalyst, the one who called other guys to see if they would show up over the holidays or during the summer when people went on vacation. He was also the spirit of the game, a gifted shit-talker who could anger someone with a cutting remark one second and have them laughing helplessly on the floor a minute later.

Summers thought that Bernard was a gift to humanity. His best friend. Their loyalty to one another was unimpeachable, ever since they met as incoming freshmen at UWB. Bernard became the leading all-time rebounder and fifth-leading scorer in the program's history, while Summers spent two years on the varsity before mysteriously leaving the school after a promising sophomore year averaging 11 points and three assists a game coming off the bench.

Bernard had texted Summers late that afternoon to let him know that he might be a little late and to start without him. Summers had asked him what was up, but Bernard wouldn't say, which Summers found odd, as they shared nearly everything.

After the last game, some of the guys headed to the bar, but Bernard's absence weighed on Summers' mind, and he decided to go home to his one-bedroom apartment in Fells Point.

16

Buck dumped himself on the front bench seat of a 1974 LTD that he used for a sofa and bed. He took a long hit from a bong and coughed half of it out in rage.

"You could fuck up a wet dream, you know that?"

"How would I know that?"

Jackie sat opposite Buck on a bean bag chair held together by duct tape. They were in Buck's current residence, an abandoned house that a friend had allowed him to stay in while the friend shacked up with his girlfriend, an arrangement that Jackie thought would be temporary if the friend was anything like Buck.

It was dark in the house, due to lack of electricity. The house, a wood-frame box with a cinder-block foundation, stood a half-block away from the nearest neighbor, from whom Buck was stealing electricity during the day. At night, they used a generator when they needed to run the space heater or use the microwave.

"Take my word for it, asshole. Shit, you fucked up my plan; my beautiful plan," Buck shaking his head in disbelief.

"If it wasn't for me, we'd have never been able to abduct Jamal to begin with. You wanted to use chloroform, which doesn't work the way you see it on TV. You coulda gotten me and Ashley killed."

"Abduct. Abduct. I'm not an educated man, but I think it's not abducting when the target is running around free."

"How do you know he's running around free? We did a two-block search. How do you know he's not lying dead in a ditch somewhere?"

"Why would he be dead? He was alive enough the last time we saw him. Alive enough that the sonuvabitch kicked your pussy butt and ran away. He's probably home by now eatin' KFC and fucking his white girlfriend."

"You don't know that. By the way, brilliant move knocking on everybody's door and claiming we were bounty hunters. Do you know what we look like compared to him, even with his hands zip-tied behind his back?"

Buck took another hit, held it for a moment and exhaled violently.

"I shoulda known not to hire a boy who loves those so-called people of color. It's a wonder you had the balls to hit the guy in the first place. Maybe you should have sent an engraved invitation with an RSVP. As for going door to door, if this was the Curtis Bay in my granddaddy's day and age that boy would be tied up in a backyard with a couple of pit bulls snacking on those $400 shoes."

"If this was your granddaddy's day and age, we couldn't have found a Black businessman in a position to be kidnapped in the first place. You just made the situation worse. You didn't realize that this neighborhood is half Black? Canvas the neighborhood? Do we look like FBI?"

"I'm not going to argue with a guy who has the street smarts of a fuckin' poodle. What do you think we should do Einstein?"

"I say we recharge his phone and check his messages. His girlfriend or someone else might have called by now. It's 10 o'clock. Maybe he was due home and the girlfriend is worried. If she calls, maybe we can say that we have him and tell her the terms of the deal. I also think we need to get away from here tonight, in case one of the neighbors that you canvassed has called the cops and they're looking for us as we speak."

"Nobody knows us in this neighborhood and if we lay low in this house they'll never find us. It's Baltimore City cops we're talkin' about; not the best and brightest. Shit, if one of them finds us, he'll probably want to get in on the deal."

"What deal? Get in on the ransom for a person we don't have in our custody? And what about the witness?" Shit, it slipped. Jackie knew he shouldn't have done the weed. It's like truth serum when he's high on good weed; not that he was ever good at hiding stuff anyway.

"Witness. What witness?"

"Well, somebody could have seen us. I mean we were only a few blocks away from the square at happy hour in Canton."

Buck put down the bong, heaved himself up from the bench seat and started pacing around the room, alternating "shit" with "fuck" and "fucking shitass shit."

"I told you if the coast wasn't clear, not to do it. We're in no hurry I told you. Now you're telling me there might, fuckin' might, be a witness? Did you see somebody?"

"I don't know...but there could have been somebody who turned the corner or something after we did our surveillance. Shit happened pretty fast once I knocked him out and got him in the trunk, but you never know."

"Surveillance? Oh, now you and Ashley are the A-Team? And 'you never know'? You fuckin' never know?" Buck's face was red verging on purple and spittle was flying everywhere. "Did the girl see anything? And where is she anyway? That's all we need is a little cokehead running off her fuckin' mouth. She'd probably do or say anything for a few lines."

"You should have thought of that before you hired her. And how should I know where she went? Where does she hang out? Did you vet her at all, other than knowing she would do something like this for an eight-ball?"

"Listen to your barrel butt. 'Vet her', as if I was hiring a fuckin' bank teller or a CIA trainee. Fuck, man, if you could take your head out of a fuckin' book once in a while maybe you'd see the real world."

"If I could handle the real world, why would I be doing this with you?"

Buck gave his best incredulous face, which looked the same as his dyspeptic face to Jackie.

"What I should have done, lard ass, is vet you. As far as I could see, the girl didn't do anything wrong. She earned her eight-ball honestly. I'd be more likely to hire her in the future than I would someone like you who loves coloreds more than people of his own race."

"I don't love your so-called coloreds more than people of our race; maybe it's just you that I don't love as much."

17

After returning home from Carmelo's game, another beat-down that seemed to have no bearing on his son's disposition or appetite for pizza, Tony kissed Lidia on the cheek and went straight into the spare bedroom he called his study. It was a small, square room with a tiny window that looked out into the side of his neighbor's house, 10 yards away.

Lidia complained about the tiny lot on which the house stood and the draftiness of the brick two-story, built in the early 50s, but this was home to Tony. He could walk to Talucci's on the corner for a beer or two, and get one of the best Italian cold cut subs in the city two blocks away at Bernardo's. Saint Matthews was less than a mile away if he decided to become a practicing Catholic again.

After getting Charlaine's call, Tony had sent a text to Jacey Creed asking for her to scan his computer at work for a third time to see if she could find out the source of the email he'd received to engage DII's services monitoring Prisha Kapoor. He also wanted to be sure that the company's system hadn't been compromised when he opened the email and clicked on the link that showed the advance payment the sender was prepared to transfer to the DII bank account. Tony thought it was another scam, but Jacey told him that it was legit, and sure enough, when Tony provided his banking account information the money appeared within a couple of hours. The agency was doing okay, but Tony sure did like the five-figure deposit.

But now he couldn't believe his apparent greed in accepting the payment at face value. For some reason, he'd let his guard slip. He wasn't sure if it was about Carmelo's impending tuition for the expensive private school in Roland Park they were going to send him to next year or figuring out how to cover the balloon mortgage contract that he signed five years ago for the place in West Ocean City, the one that started at three percent and had swelled to nine percent. At least the place was increasing in value and Tony could dump it if he got in a financial bind, although it would break Lidia's heart and make Tony forever yearn for those tan lines above her tart red nipples. She could always get her sun from the back patio, but as Lidia pointed out, the view of the Langley's backyard, with that '57 Ford pickup that's been up on cinder blocks for the last two years and the rusted swing set that's been out of service since the Langley twins turned 12, isn't exactly the eggshell-colored sand and pounding blue waters of Ocean City.

Jacey told Tony that she could uncover the email sender's IP address and track it back to a geographical location and a domain name, but that would probably not get them to the source of the email, as people sending anonymous messages use a proxy or gateway to hide their whereabouts. Connections made using certain routers go through several computers around the world before reaching their destination. Each step is encrypted so the path cannot be traced and the source cannot be identified.

Tony often thought that computer networks giveth and taketh away: For all of the benefits they provide for tracking information they can also be an insidious tool for hiding identities and sending investigators down false trails.

Tony was also a bit wary about the unfettered access to the company's computer systems that he gave Jacey. She'd worked for him for three years and had done nothing to suggest that she was not trustworthy, but Tony still didn't like one person holding all the keys to a computer network that contained a lot of secrets. Sometimes he longed for the days of the locked safe or file cabinet. He had a friend in the business who refused to use computers or cell phones and leveraged that fact as a marketing tactic. Some people passed the guy off as a conspiracy nut, but he got some good accounts by assuring people that their information would never be exposed to a hard drive, the Internet, or the digital cloud.

If nothing could be done to get to the source of the email, Tony thought he could work on finding out who might have hired him by gathering information on all the top people at 3Make, thinking about what motive they might have had in hiring his agency and whether they could have something to do with the abduction of Bernard Jamal. He didn't worry about digging into Jamal's background and whereabouts: He knew Charlaine would be relentless on that front. If Jamal was still alive and in Baltimore or anywhere in the country for that matter, she'd track him.

Beyond understanding what was happening with 3Make, Tony had some other issues etching at the back of his mind. He worried that he might have lost the trust of his best investigator. He knew a bunch of other agencies, in Baltimore and beyond, were after Charlaine and could offer more money than he could. What he offered were intangibles: good benefits, better working hours, a convivial workplace, a trusting environment. But, he had done something to undermine the last benefit. He had to set the situation straight and promise that it would never happen again. He was also thinking that he needed someone to help him vet clients. He was thinking about asking Charlaine if she would help him on the management end, maybe as his first vice president. But, she might not want more responsibility. Tony had good people in the past to whom he wanted to give a bigger management role, but they turned him down: Who wants to go through the shit he goes through every day for an extra $10,000 a year?

18

Kensey Mathers stirred in her bed, flinging her left hand behind her, expecting it to land on Bernard's rock-hard shoulder. Instead it hit an empty pillow.

They'd been living together for four years. It was serious for both of them, but they were in no hurry to marry. Both thought a relationship didn't need a piece of paper to give it legitimacy. She trusted him and he showed no reason for her not to.

They were different in almost every way except where it counts: What they thought about people and the respect that should be accorded them. They thought that people matter more than institutions. That there is intrinsic good in the world, but it's not always easy to find. That most people do the best they can, but there are some who'll never get it. They thought that time is non-linear and knows no structure: Your parents, aunts, uncles, grandparents are always alive within you and can be summoned at times to provide succor or even practical advice. They valued honesty, caring and trust.

Kensey tried going back to sleep, but tossed about in the sheets until she slung her legs to the side of the bed, slowly tested her bum knee, and shuffled into the living room. She couldn't imagine where Bernard would be at 1 a.m. on a weeknight. He usually played at Farley for a couple of hours and then stopped for a beer or two, getting home by 11 at the latest. She picked up her phone to call him, but it went to an automated message that his mailbox was full. *Shit, Bernard, I told you about that last week. What if I needed you? And goddammit, I need to get to work in the morning, and so do you. We're not fucking kids anymore.*

She didn't want to be awake. She had to make a presentation to a potential client tomorrow. John Summers had recommended that Kensey pitch PR services for Scan2CAD, the company for which he worked as marketing director. Scan2CAD developed software that turns 3D scans into functional CAD files for building objects of almost any size or dimensions. The company was growing rapidly, adding 30 employees, mostly engineers, in the last 11 months. The account would be small to begin with, but had the potential to be much larger, as venture capital firms were wooing the owners, a husband and wife team who considered themselves serial entrepreneurs. Summers would be part of the team that qualified the PR applicants, but ultimately it would be the owners' decision.

Kensey was excited when the opportunity came, but now frazzled. *Fuck, Bern, where are you?* When they'd talked before about him not calling he laughed it off, asking what did she think could happen to him? He never felt any apprehension about anything; not that he showed, anyway. She didn't know how he gained that confidence, growing up where he did, but it was always there, like that white spot on the left front of his modified afro.

19

J ackie put together the two bean bag chairs that served as his bed and tried to sleep. He was comfortable enough but too tired. At least his body was. His brain was something else altogether. Racing like a gerbil on its caged wheel. He'd been low before, but never like this. Falling in with a racist like Buck who doesn't give a damn about a human life.

There was a corner of his brain that Jackie reserved for empathy, and despite his best efforts he couldn't eradicate it for Buck. That racism didn't come from thin air. Nor did Buck's nostalgia for a part of the city his family moved away from when he was five. In its early days, Curtis Bay was part of the dream. Blue-collar white people with jobs, cars, self-respect. Owning the city, with its Baltimore Colts corrals in all the bars, Brooks Robinson holding down the hot corner, coddies for 50 cents each at the Previs Brothers counter in the Fells Point market. Fells Point when it was still raw, its oysters and its residents. Looks like a citified version of Disney now. Used to be drunks lying in the doorways on Sunday morning. Now you had to dodge joggers pushing strollers that look like mini Mercedes.

Goddamn this city makes for misshapen dreams and handy scapegoats. Buck yearning for the city where you could go crabbing off the piers, have a block party over pit beef, oysters and Natty Boh. All that crashing down in Buck's mind because of the coloreds, the elitist fairies, the corrupt politicos. Jackie could understand some of it. He wouldn't be surprised if Curtis Bay becomes the new Canton, or like that National Harbor in PG

County, full of hotels, condos, fine dining and bars that people like Buck and Jackie couldn't afford. Cities where people lived, worked, drank and socialized in the corner bars and back alleys had turned into playgrounds for the rich. They'd probably give Curtis Bay a new name, like Prosperity Point or some other bullshit. Jackie hated what was happening as much as Buck, but he didn't blame it on any type of people; he blamed it on corporate greed. Big business. The wealthy wanting to own everything desirable. Not leaving a sliver of the cake for common folks.

Jackie was tired of fighting. Tired of trying to get his nibble. Tired of hurting nearly every damn minute of his life until the pills kicked in. And not even the pills satisfied him anymore, making him stupid and resentful. The pain. It was back now, gnawing at his left knee and working its way up to his groin. His swollen wrist pulsing like an overwrought hose. The weed and bourbon had kept it at bay, but parts of his body were now checking in to remind Jackie that he was a broken-down man.

Broken down or not, he had to get outta here. Buck could have killed Jamal if he could shoot straight. And what would stop him from abducting someone else? In Buck's mind, Jackie had screwed up a great plan. He would likely try again and this time maybe with a more manageable target. There were plenty of villains in Buck's world and he could justify torturing or killing any one of them: women, gays, trans, Hispanics—like fish in a fuckin' barrel as Buck would say.

Jackie looked over at Buck, snorting in his sleep, with his wallet, keys and money on the floor beside the LTD bench seat. He could just split now. Grab whatever money Buck had on the floor and take off with the Town Car. Head to Virginia or PA. Nobody can connect him to this except for Buck and Ashley, and he was pretty sure that they didn't even know his full name. Jamal and that Black woman witness might be able to describe him, but that's about it. He'd have to ditch the Town Car fairly quickly, but tomorrow would be soon enough, and he could be in Jersey or North

Cackalacky by then. You could probably sell a car easily in either of those places, no questions asked.

But first the pain. Jackie had a small stash he'd gotten from a dealer on the street near Lexington Market. He had some doubts but the guy said, "You could become a regular by the looks of you. Why would I give you something that would do harm? This is prime pharmaceutical shit." Jackie saw other guys waiting nearby so said what the fuck. He fingered the bag in his jacket pocket and pulled out two pills. They were legit. R|P inscribed on one side and the number 5 overtop 325 on the other side. Same as the ones he was once prescribed.

Jackie popped the pills, crushing them with his teeth and swallowing hard, the acrid taste filling his mouth. He tiptoed over to Buck's side, looked him in the face to make sure he was asleep, and grabbed his wallet, cash and keys, tip-toeing out of the house in his stocking feet. He startled when the door creaked but kept going, carrying his shoes in one hand and holding the car keys in the other. He put on his shoes while sitting on the narrow wooden steps leading up to the back door. He tiptoed over to the car and after a moment of panic, the door combination for the Town Car came back to him. He quickly entered it and slid into the front seat. *Please start*, he whispered, and turned the key, welcoming the blissful sound of the V8 burbling to life.

Jackie turned right out of the driveway, opened the driver's side window and threw Buck's phone in front of the car. When he heard a satisfying crunch of plastic under his back tire, he knew he had made the right move. He was exhilarated; in the moment but also dreaming. Dreaming of Sparrows Point, riding his bike alongside the boulevard and turning off into that little side street, Lakeview Ave., no lake at all, but dead ending at Jones Creek, now nearly clear and healthy after a century of toxic sludge, like a 90-year-old who smoked for 89 years and now has remarkably clear lungs. Nature performs those miracles daily and in plentitude, until it gets tired of our shit.

Jackie would go down Lakeview to the pier where the crabbing boats came in just before suppertime. He'd chat with Captain Jack and help the crabbers offload their catch. They didn't need his help, but they were tired after a long day and if it was a good one, they'd throw some bills Jackie's way, and maybe a few stray crabs, which Jackie's mother would steam and put in soup or flake the flesh into some farm-fresh succotash in a cream sauce. In her earlier years his mom was a waitress in many fine establishments (as she called them) in New Orleans and Charleston, and she paid attention to the workings of the kitchen. On a rare day off, she'd get to the restaurant early, watch the line cooks break down chickens and fish, hang out in the back of the kitchen and stay out of the way as things heated up. The teamwork, petty grudges, grinding routines, command hierarchy, good graces and bad felt like a concentration of life itself. She told Jackie about all of it, sipping on an ever-present rum and coke and stepping out every hour or so to do something else out of sight.

Jackie could rattle some pots and pans himself. Maybe he'd head to Charleston and catch on with a restaurant, kicking the oxy and starting fresh. He knew the pay was shit, but he didn't need much. Get a day off now and then and head to the beach. There was Folly Beach with those weather-beaten wooden houses and butterflies everywhere. Jackie could see them now, flying around his head, surrounding him like he was a prince. Then they started blanketing him, fluttering all over his face, into his mouth and his nostrils until he gasped for breath, feeling a sudden chill even though the heater had warmed the Town Car like a freshly stoked fire.

Jackie pulled the car to the curb near the entrance of an abandoned warehouse. So tired. Cold. Breath shallow and seeking oxygen. He searched for the window button, but couldn't find it. *Gotta get some air. Free air. Anywhere air.* Banging at the window with floppy fists. Getting weak. *Just lay down on the bench seat and relax a bit. No need to panic. Just a little nap, little nap, little nap.*

20

"Shit!"

Joe pounded his beer down on the TV table so hard that a wave of brew squirted from the top of the can. "My kingdom for a three-point specialist," he muttered. The Wiz had lost another one because they couldn't hit big shots down the stretch. Their star, Bradley Beal, was shooting just over 26% from three-point land and there was no one on the team connecting on more than 35% of his threes. Joe liked the way they played under Wes Unseld's son, but they needed more reliable long-distance guns.

Joe heard some soft mumbling from the sofa and turned to see the Doctor blinking his eyes open, then shutting them in pain.

"Hey, Doctor, did you say something?" Joe asked. He thought the big guy said something about summer. The dude's eyes opened a bit more and squinched closed again.

"Summers. Need Summers,"

"You dreaming, son?"

Bernard tried lifting his head, winced again, and closed his eyes. "Need my boy Summers," he whispered.

"Take it easy, big man. Let me get you a drink of old H^{2}O. Unless you need something stronger."

Bernard sat up slowly, resting his hands on either side of his jaw and his elbows on his knees. He moved his head back and forth to loosen a kink in his neck, his eyes struggling to open.

"You gotta lump on the noggin', a swollen ankle, and some wrist scrapes from these here ties," said Joe, holding up the plastic restraints he'd cut off. "There were two white boys going door to door searching for you. Something about jumpin' bail, but you don't look the type. I've been calling you Dr. J."

Bernard smiled then closed his eyes in pain again.

"Where am I?"

"You in Curtis Bay, son, south Baltimore, the land of peasant living," said Joe, chuckling.

"What am I doing here?"

"You were running away from those white boys and wound up on my doorstep. What were those boys doing to you? Rough-looking boys. One seemed okay, but the other had murder in his eyes."

Bernard placed fingertips on his eyelids and moved them back and forth, lightly massaging his eyeballs.

"What would they want with me?"

"Precisely my question. You do something to get under their skin?"

"I don't think I even know them, much less get under their skin. I don't run with that kind of crowd anymore."

Joe nodded his head in agreement.

"I didn't think so, but there they was chasing you down. Come to my door looking for you. Even if I knew your whereabouts, I wouldn't have told those boys. They're looking for trouble."

Bernard patted his front and back pockets.

"My phone's gone. So's my wallet and money. You think they just wanted to rob me?"

"Well, I'm no Easy Rawlins, but they had more in mind than robbery. If it was just that, they wouldn't be trying to relocate your Black ass."

"Easy who?"

"You know, the detective in the Walter Mosley books. Thought everybody knew Easy. 'Devil in the Blue Dress'?"

"Denzel and Cheadle?"

"Yeah, the movie. You got it. Damn good version. What do you remember?"

"Last thing was meeting with a business colleague, Prisha, at Formosa in Canton. Prisha works for a company I'm funding."

"Funding? You rich, son? Maybe that's why they wanted you. Tried to kidnap you, maybe. Could have picked a smaller target, but they didn't exactly seem like phi beta kappa material."

"I'm not that rich, but I'm VP of a venture capital company, so I might be wealthy eventually, if I keep getting lucky."

"You look familiar. You play ball?"

"I'm Bernard Jamal. I played at UWB and a couple of years in Poland."

"Hmmm, might have read about you in the *Sunpapers*. Where'd you go to high school?"

"City College, sir, the thrill on the hill."

"Sheeet. You mean the dump on the hump? My boy went to Southern. What are you doing in Curtis Bay, son? Doesn't exactly seem like your territory. Didn't seem like the white boys' territory either. We're mostly old folks here, except for the gangs with their clubhouses and shit."

"You see anyone else except the white dudes? I have a vague notion of someone else, maybe a girl."

"You keep thinking on it and maybe it'll come back to you."

But then the guy called Bernard fluttered his eyes and fell to his side on the couch. Joe placed his head gingerly on the pillow and lifted his legs back up on the sofa. He'd give him a bit more time to rest and meanwhile try to find out some more about Bernard Jamal. He went to the kitchen where his iPad was charging, unplugged it, and carried it out to the living room, where Bernard was snoring softly. Joe wasn't the most computer literate guy in the world, but he knew how to do a productive search and it took only five minutes to come up with the *Sun* article on Bernard Jamal and his venture capital firm, TripleDouble. Joe didn't know much about the venture capital business, but he knew those white boys weren't any kind of tech guys, more like your run-of-the-mill thugs.

The ice had melted in the two towels applied to Bernard's wounds, so Joe went out to the kitchen and placed them on the oven handle to dry. He took two more fresh tea towels off the shelf, got some more ice out of the freezer and went to work again with the rolling pin, visions of Dinah flashing through his mind.

Whaddaya know, thought Joe, *I have a real live mystery on my hands.*

It was about 3 a.m. when Bernard stirred again. Joe had fallen asleep watching reruns of Mannix on one of those oldies networks when he heard the big man groan. Joe was a light sleeper, especially when he nodded off on his BarcaLounger.

"He lives!"

"Where am I?"

"In a safe place, Youngblood, a safe place."

"I thank you, I think, but what am I doing here?"

"I'll explain it to you again. The short version. But first, how about a drink? A beer or Hennessy? You might need something when I start telling you what I know about your current shituation."

"I'll go with the hard stuff, but I better drink fast. I have a feeling I have some explaining to do to my girlfriend."

"I think she'll be sympathetic once I vouch for the circumstances surrounding your evident disappearance."

"Evident disappearance? Are you an ex-cop?"

"No, but I read a lot about cops, if that helps."

Joe rose slowly from the BarcaLounger and walked to the kitchen while explaining again to Bernard what happened to him. When Joe was done, Bernard asked him if he could use his phone. Joe handed over the old iPhone 6; he didn't think it was old, but everyone else evidently did. According to the stuff he read in the *Sun* and online, he should have gone through at least two newer phones by now.

Bernard picked up the phone, frowned at it, then nodded his head in relief when he remembered Kensey's phone number. He never realized how much he relied on the contact and recent call lists when using the phone. He was lucky if he remembered his own number. Hmmm, his own number. That gave him an idea. But first Kensey.

She answered on the first ring.

"Please tell me you're okay, Bernard, and why I shouldn't kill you if you are."

"I'm sorry, Kens, if I coulda I woulda called you. I'm going to put on a man named Joe Monroe who can explain it better than I can at this point."

"Miss Kensey, this is Joe. Your boyfriend's safe in my house in Curtis Bay. He has a nasty bump on his temple, a swolled-up ankle, and some other bumps and bruises, but he's generally okay. He doesn't remember what happened to him after he left a bar in Canton, but here's what I know."

Joe told the story for the third time; he was getting good at chiseling it down to the essentials, what he imagined Mosley did when he was editing the first draft of one of his crime novels. When he was done, Kensey thanked him and Joe handed the phone back to Bernard.

Kensey's voice was a combination of tired, relieved and pissed.

"You're a lucky man, you know that?"

"Yeah, I guess you could say that. At least I'm not taking a dirt nap."

"You certainly sound cool about it."

"I could get more hysterical if you think it would help."

"I think what would help would be for me to talk with someone else who loves you and might be worried. I think I'll call Summers; he texted me tonight asking if you were home, but I was already in bed trying to get a good night's sleep before the presentation tomorrow, or this morning since it's now three fucking 15. I tried calling you, but it went to messaging and then your box was full."

"Damn, I'd forgotten about your pitch tomorrow...I mean today. Can you postpone?"

"I could if you need me, but I don't want to. I don't want to lie and I don't want to tell the truth: They might think I live an unstable life. Summers told me there are already a few people who are wary of me because I'm a friend of his. I don't want to give them anything they might hold against me. Do you need me to come and pick you up and maybe help you find your car?"

"No, baby, you concentrate on the pitch. I know you'll kill, no matter what your state of mind or the lack of sleep. I've heard many of these agency pitches and you're in another league, like LeBron playing against college kids."

"That's nice of you, but you haven't seen me this morning. I look like Rocky Raccoon after a weekend bender."

"Take a nice cold shower. Couple cups of coffee. If you need to reach me, call on Joe's phone. We're going to go over a few things and map out a course of action. I don't want to call in anyone else until I have more information. The shit's just not adding up at the moment and I'm hoping something will jog my memory."

"Joe's a fuckin' saint; tell him that, but maybe leave out the fuckin'. And shit, B, be careful, be very careful. I need you, baby."

"Yeah, I'll tell Joe, and I'll be careful. It'd kill me if I missed out on a long life with you."

"You could have phrased it better, but your heart is in the right place. Just keep it beating, okay?"

"That's my number one goal. Love you, baby. Break a leg."

"I love you, and don't break a leg."

When Bernard hung up he thought about tracking his phone. If the guys who knocked him out and kidnapped him were still in possession of it, he might be able to find out their location and go after them. Bernard was technologically astute, but he didn't pay much attention to his phone's settings. He thought it was a long shot but he asked Joe about it.

Joe answered excitedly.

"Good idea, Youngblood. Do you have the Find My setting on?"

Bernard's face dropped.

"No, Joe. Now that you mention it, I remember changing that setting. There's a lot of competition among VCs and when I'm recruiting a new company to fund I don't want the possibility of anyone knowing where I'm located at any given time."

"Then I don't think we can track the phone, Blood. At least I can't. Maybe the cops could."

Bernard shook his head.

"I'm not ready to call in the police just yet."

"It's your show, son. Here's another idea. How about we go gumshoe? They're likely in the neighborhood and there aren't that many houses around here anymore. We could drive around a bit and see if you recognize anything."

"Sounds like a plan, Joe."

A few minutes later, Joe came out of a back room and placed a small revolver in Bernard's hand and put a larger one in the front pocket of his leather jacket.

"I don't know how you feel about weapons, Doctor J, but we're in some shaky territory here and I don't want them boys to have an undue advantage. Treat that piece kindly; it was my wife Dinah's favorite."

21

Buck woke up shivering from the cold that had set in during the night. He hadn't run the space heater because he was afraid that a neighbor might hear the generator. That possibility didn't bother him before, but he was starting to get paranoid. It was that fuckin' Jackie, always bringing up shit that might happen. Buck picked up his jacket that had fallen off his shoulders and secured it around his neck.

He was falling back asleep when he heard a phone ringing. Who the fuck would call at this hour? Probably one of Jackie's PTSD pals, all of those losers crying about how much they hurt all the time and can't get any sleep; calling one another to see if their buddy can help them score or front them a few pills to get through the day or night.

Buck hated opioids. Killing white kids from the burbs and the sticks who never had access to the heavy shit before. It wasn't their classmates, the Opies and Karens of the world, bringing in that shit. It was coming in from New York via some kind of Mexican pipeline, flowing over that border that Trump tried to seal off but the pussy Democrats want to keep open so those wetbacks can come in and take our jobs, rape our women, use our hospitals and schools that we pay for with our taxes.

Jackie tried to tell him one time about the dreamers, how they work and pay taxes. Model fuckin' citizens, except they ain't, are they? Buck didn't give a shit about legal status, he just wanted them out of here. This is a white fuckin' country from the constitution days. He never read the constitution, but people have told him enough about it that he knows. Knows more about it than guys like Jackie, who're always twisting it into some liberal bullshit. The same people who twist Trump's words against him. The same fuckers who don't honor the bible and say that Jesus would welcome fags, lesbos and trans. Those assholes who say we ain't born man or woman; that we can find out we're a different sex when we're 13 or 14, or even 40 or 50. Why would God do that shit? Why would he create you one way just so you could change it?

That phone ringing was like a needle in Buck's skull. Why wasn't Jackie picking up? He rolled over and saw that the bean bags were pressed up against one another but there was no Jackie. Probably one of what he called "his insomnia episodes." Insomnia, another crock of shit.

"Answer the phone, faggot!"

Crickets. Buck's head was bursting. He jerked fully awake and stood up, dizzy from the booze, weed and blow. He looked around in the dark and didn't see that fat fuck Jackie. He looked down on the floor where he thought he put his wallet, phone and cash and they weren't there. Maybe he put them on the table, but when he shuffled over there he didn't see them.

"Jackie! Where the fuck are you?"

Still no answer, but the phone had stopped ringing. Buck picked up a flashlight but the battery was low and the light was weak. Then he saw it, perched on the edge of a chair near the door, where Jackie must have set it. But it wasn't Jackie's phone and it wasn't his; it must be Jamal's. Someone was trying to contact him. Buck picked up the phone and looked at the Recents list. It read "Summers," the friend Buck had read about in the *Sun* article. He turned the phone off, walked over to the window overlooking the backyard, and parted the sheets serving as curtains.

"Fuckin' shit; fuckin' shit!" The Town Car was gone, along with Jackie no doubt. Buck stomped on the wood floor until it nearly cracked and paced in circles around the disheveled room.

He needed to keep his shit together. That's what smart people do. *Okay, assess the situation.* His phone, wallet and cash are gone. Replaceable losses. Jackie is gone. Also replaceable. He couldn't see Jackie going far. If he had somewhere better to go than Baltimore he would have gone there by now, rather than living the day-to-day scramble of the life he has here. The car? Buck had stolen that five days ago from a former friend who'd fucked him on a coke deal. The guy might be looking for it, but Buck doubted it, since the guy probably stole it to begin with or got it from a chop shop. And if he's looking for it now, he'll find Jackie or someone else has it, so Buck is free and clear. He can always get another car.

He probably should get out of this house now. Number one, his neighbor might catch on that Buck has been siphoning his electricity. In this neighborhood, that's grounds for a shooting or ass whipping. Number two, there's Jackie driving around in that Town Car and his hints about a possible witness to the kidnapping. If Jackie gets caught, he'll snitch to save his own ass. Number three, Jamal might have location tracking on his phone and already has identified Buck's whereabouts.

Buck thought about calling his own phone to see if Jackie or someone else picks up. He was nervous about his phone being out there somewhere, as there were text messages that could incriminate him. He'd been to Jessup once, on felony grand theft auto charges for 16 months, and vowed never to return. Nothing terrible happened to him, but the day-to-day fear left him sleeping only a few hours a night. The Aryan Brotherhood looked after him a little, but he had to pay for the protection, either with drugs or money, until he was broke and in debt to every contact he had on the outside.

Buck wondered if he could track the location of his own phone. That might lead him to Jackie. He didn't know if he had location turned on or not. He never consciously turned it off, but really didn't know how to use it. He decided to give it a try, taking Jamal's phone and dialing his number, which he barely remembered. The phone rang eight times then went to messages. After the prompt, Buck spat into the phone.

"Are you there, Jackie? Listen here you fat fuck. Return the car, my phone, wallet and money, and we'll consider this a mistake. In case you forget, we're in this together, and I've done nothing illegal so far—my word against yours. Remember, you're the one who knocked the boy out and put him in the trunk. That's assault and battery, fat boy, not to mention attempted kidnapping. So take the easy way out and return my shit, right away."

Jamal had a newer model of iPhone. Of course he would. All these executives love the Apple shit. Probably bought a new model each year. Buck had a four-year-old Android phone, nearly the most basic model you could find. He didn't have time to waste on those apps like Facebook, Instagram, TikTok or those stupid games Jackie played, his neck permanently bent from looking down at that tiny screen in his huge hands. But then Buck saw the Uber logo and it gave him an idea: He'd use the phone to hail an Uber and then get rid of it. Or maybe he didn't have to get rid of it.

Jackie once called Buck some kind of name—luddie or something like that—making fun of him because he didn't know one of the phone features. But Buck was no idiot; he knew the basic shit and how to google what he didn't know. He did a search and within minutes found the Location Services setting and saw that Jamal had turned it off. Wonderful. Buck loved technology, as long as it worked on his terms. He went into the Uber app and scheduled a ride to his cousin's house. The map showed a driver was 10 minutes away. Just enough time for Buck to gather up his shit and get his head straight.

22

Charlaine woke up at 7 a.m. tangled in the sheets, the smell of freshly brewed coffee tickling her nostrils. She'd only slept four hours or so but felt refreshed with what was her drug of choice: knowledge. Baltimore's Greek Freak was Bernard Jamal and he was linked closely to 3Make through his venture capital firm that was providing a large chunk of the company's funding for new product development.

Bernard Jamal was not your typical venture capitalist. He didn't have a banking background, hadn't founded any technology companies himself, nor did he come from big money. He majored in urban planning at UWB and wanted to continue along that path according to the story in the *Sun*, until he teamed up with John Summers. The two friends invested all of their savings and contributions from friends and family in a reverse engineering service network that did nearly all of its commerce digitally, parceling out the work to subcontractors that were certified and regulated by the parent company. It was basically a McDonalds for small- to medium-sized engineering and manufacturing projects. It is now worth millions.

Summers went on to head marketing for a 3D scanning start-up, while Jamal continued looking for new opportunities; the first a niche operation that produced 3D-printed parts on demand for NASCAR and later Formula 1 teams, then a gaming company with interactive engine technology that could be used for virtual reality training and engineering simulations.

According to the *Sun* article, 3Make is the biggest play yet for Jamal's firm, called TripleDouble. He's partnered with John Mesceri, a local guy who inherited a fortune from his father's syndicated car wash business. It's generally thought that Mesceri is the big money guy and Jamal is the go-getter, the linchpin that finds the opportunities and brings together the key technology players with the money people. According to the article, Jamal was a hands-on VC who likes to know as much as possible about the operation of every start-up in which TripleDouble invests: the people, the technology, the processes, the competition, the potential for scaling and growth.

Charlaine answered a lot of her own questions with her google research, but, as always, the answers begat more questions. As she showered, the water sluicing over her body, she couldn't come to grips with the scenario that went down in Canton. She could understand why Jamal might be meeting with the CFO of the company in which he has invested heavily. But she couldn't understand how he would be involved with the bear-like guy and the Lucy sprite. Maybe it was something personal. Charlaine had read about his live-in partner in the *Sun* article. Could he have done something so heinous that an otherwise average woman would seek out thugs to plan an abduction? Where would she make such contacts?

What Charlaine had learned through her investigative and life experience was never to assume. If she had assumed that Joy was just another white girl from the suburbs they'd never have embarked on this relationship, the most precious thing in Charlaine's life. She had faith in Joy and sometimes in a nebulous God to which she prayed sporadically, but nothing much else. She'd learned that the best thing for her is to not extrapolate; to take things as they come and not make them conform to some preformed plan or perception. That didn't mean she thought things were always what they seemed; there were always things under the surface that weren't what they appeared to be. Her job, in her work and life, was to uncover everything relevant and bring it to light.

Despite the murkiness of the 3Make situation, Charlaine was excited. If she had a brain scan right now her hypothalamus would have been lit up like the pinball machines she used to play when she hung out in the Fells Point bars. After toweling off, Charlaine changed into her tailored sweats, put on her Ravens cap over her short afro, pulled on a pair of ankle socks, laced up her Skechers and headed downstairs. When she turned the corner into the kitchen there was Joy, with that smile, the smile that made Charlaine think that things might be alright.

23

As Bernard waited for Joe to unlock the passenger-side door of his Honda CRV, he gazed out into the street that intersected with the alley in back of Joe's house. He saw a Lincoln Town Car with a trail of exhaust leaking out into the cold early morning air. Joe was unlocking the car when Bernard called out to him.

"Joe. Have you seen that Town Car before?"

"Can't say I have, but it's not unusual to see a car parked there and a lot of those Lincolns are still 'round and about. That's a nice one. Kids park sometimes on that dead-end street, makin' out or smokin' weed."

"It seems familiar to me."

"Well, let's check it out big mon. But better have that piece handy. Some of these boys will cap you for lookin' at them the wrong way."

"Alright, I'll check out the driver's side and you go around to the passenger side. Okay?"

"Sounds good, Blood, but keep your hand on that piece and try not to shoot your dick off."

The two started walking toward the Town Car, slowly, due to a combination of Joe's arthritis and Bernard's sprained ankle. Bernard reached the car first, standing a foot away from the window on the driver's side and keeping a grip on the butt of the revolver in his right-hand pocket. Slumped on the bench-style seat was a huge man, probably 6'4" or so and to the heavy side of 350 pounds. Bernard tapped on the driver's side window and yelled at him.

"Heh, man. Are you okay?"

Joe recognized the man immediately. He could see part of his face from the passenger side window and it didn't look good: A bluish tint to his cheeks and his lips puffy and purple. Joe let out a low whistle.

"This is one of the boys who was chasing after you, Doctor. The boy's OD'd if you ask me. We gotta try to help him. I got some of that Narcan spray they were giving out at the community center. Those opioid ODs becoming as common as weeds around these parts. I'll also get something to bust open one of these winders."

"Okay, but we might not need to bust a window, Joe. Something's coming to me."

Joe started across the street and entered the alley behind his house with surprising quickness, Bernard watching the old man with admiration.

Ever since he was a child, Bernard had a great visual memory for numbers. He could see a batting or scoring average or an economic statistic in an article and it stuck indelibly in his memory. In this case, five numbers were appearing in his head, hand-written on a small piece of rumpled paper. He tried them out on the keyless door lock but they didn't work. Then he tried again, thinking the three in his mind might have been an eight. He re-entered the combination and there was a click. He pulled the handle of the car door and it opened.

Bernard leaned into the car and shook the guy's huge thigh, but he didn't stir. He turned off the car engine and the radio and thought he could hear some faint breathing. He tried to roll him over on his back but the guy was a load and a half. He unlocked all the doors and walked around to the passenger-side door. Bernard pressed his fingers against the side of the guy's neck and thought he could feel a faint pulse. A moment later, Joe appeared at Bernard's side with the inhaler.

"Okay, let's see if we can turn this big sonuvabitch over and I'll get some of this Narcan into his nose," said Joe, breathing heavily in the cold air.

Bernard moved the bench seat back all the way, and Joe and he kneeled in front of the big man. On the count of three they managed to heave him onto his back, his legs extending out the open driver's side door.

"You've done this before?" asked Bernard, as Joe stooped over the big guy's head with the spray bottle in his hand.

"No, but I've watched the videos. Don't know how far gone he is or if it's an opioid OD, but we'll give it a try. How'd you get the door open?"

"I remembered the combination. This is the car they used to abduct me and he's the guy who knocked me out."

"Okay. We'll deal with any—retribution or whatever—after we see if we can save his ass."

Bernard tilted the guy's head back and Joe hovered over him, placing the nozzle of the inhaler in his right nostril and pushing down the plunger. The big man groaned and starting gasping. Within seconds his eyes opened and he was staring at the ceiling of the car. He shook his head and looked up at Joe.

"What the…" he rasped, but Joe shushed him.

"Just take your time, big boy, take your time and breathe."

Joe and Bernard moved away to let the giant get his bearings. Joe put his right hand into his pocket and placed his palm on the butt of the revolver. He felt a strange sympathy for the guy but he wasn't going to take any chances. After a minute or two of wheezing, the big guy sat up in the front seat and scanned his surroundings, like a child entering a playground for the first time.

"Easy now, son," said Joe in a soothing, mild tone. "We think you OD'd on somethin' and I just gave you a dose of that there Narcan. You ain't going to do anything stupid now, are you? If you can just relax a bit, we'll get you to a hospital. No need to call the police unless my colleague here thinks it's necessary."

"No, I don't think it's necessary, at least not until we get him stabilized and talk to him a bit. You agree, big man?"

That's when Jackie turned to his left and saw Bernard Jamal staring him in the face. Jackie shook his head as if to wake from a dream, a bad one.

"No. I'm done with all of that shit. You have another dose in case I go under again?" Like a lot of opioid abusers, Jackie knew all about Narcan and how it works.

"Yeah, I got you covered," said Joe. "We're going to get you in the back of this car and take you to the emergency room at Medstar Harbor. I hope you ain't offended by my colleague holding a gun on you, just in case."

"Seems fair to me," muttered Jackie, "given the circumstances."

Joe and Bernard moved to the driver's side of the car and each took hold of one of the big guy's ankles, which were the size of a grapefruit. They heaved simultaneously and moved him about six inches, repeating the procedure until they got him to the edge of the door and were able to plant his feet on the street pavement.

"If we grab your arms, think you can stand?" asked Joe.

"Yeah, I think so, but my left knee hurts like a bitch."

"Alright then. I'll get on the right side and Bernard here will be on the left just in case you need to lean in that direction. You know Bernard, I presume."

"Yes, yes. I'm sorry Bernard. I know you're a good dude. You have every right to leave me here to die."

"Nobody's dying here, man," said Bernard, hoping his ankle would hold up if the guy leaned his way. "What's your name?"

"Jackie Reynolds, Jr."

"Sounds familiar."

"I was at UWB when you were. Football."

"Alright you two," said Joe. "We can have a reunion later. Let's get to the hospital and then Bernard and I can come back and get your partner. What's his name?"

"Buck, Buck Boyd."

"Sounds like a stone-cold redneck," said Joe. "OK, we're going to help you stand, then get you to the backseat where we'll lie you down again. You sure you're not going to do anything stupid? We're both armed, so if you get one of us, the other will cap your ass. You're not exactly a small target."

"No, I'm cool. I'm on your side."

Bernard passed his hand over his left temple and winced.

"Coulda fooled me. Now let's do this on three."

Bernard counted off and they brought Jackie to his feet, where he tipped face forward until Bernard braced himself against him to stop any further momentum. Joe and Bernard wrapped the guy's huge arms around each of their shoulders and hobbled him to the open back door. From there they pushed him ass-first into the backseat.

"Shit," said Joe, "next time get abducted by a smaller motherfucker, OK?"

Joe got in the driver's seat and moved the bench seat forward until Bernard's knees were nearly touching the glove box.

"Sorry, but I couldn't reach the pedals otherwise, and we don't need to add a vehicular accident to all the other shit."

"I'm good," said Bernard, "but if you move it up any farther I'll be kissing the windshield." He reluctantly took out Dinah's revolver from his pocket and hefted it in his palm, casually aiming it at Jackie's chest. "Now, let's go over a few things, Mr. Reynolds Jr., offensive lineman." Because Bernard remembered him now; a more fit, baby-faced version, always ready with a smile. How could he have dropped so far so quickly? *No need to wonder*, thought Bernard, *this is Baltimore*.

Jackie started telling the story haltingly, needing to stop for frequent deep breaths. He told them everything he could remember at the moment. How he met Buck at a Narcotics Anonymous meeting that they had to attend as part of a parole agreement. Buck was arrested when a routine traffic stop for a supposedly stolen car led to the cops uncovering a crack pipe with residue. Jackie was taken in for a forged oxy script. Neither had any intention of coming clean. After the mandated meetings, they'd go to a local bar across the street from the church basement. Jackie didn't like all the racist shit from Buck, but he did relate to his fall from grace, such as it was. Buck wasn't an athlete, but a once-promising pianist who lost his desire to practice three or four hours a day. The quick score was way more satisfying and profitable. Besides, Buck didn't like music of any kind, a cruel trick given his natural aptitude with the piano.

Bernard and Joe stayed mostly silent while Jackie unraveled his story, Bernard still holding the gun loosely in the massive palm of his hand and Joe snorting a few times in derision as Jackie related Buck's theory of coloreds and gays ruining everything that was good about Baltimore. As they turned into the hospital entrance Joe offered up his summation of the matter.

"Boy, I'm tempted to just say you's a stupid motherfucker, but I seen what those opioids can do to a person. I think inside you might be an OK man if you can get that shit out of your system. Maybe you got somethin' to offer other men like you. But this Buck boy, he probably ain't redeemable, at least not by the likes of the Maryland penal system. We'll get you checked in and then we'll go back and see about him. You said you have his wallet. Hand it over to Bernard here. Is your, what do you call it, accomplice, staying in Curtis Bay?"

Jackie grunted and reached into his jacket pocket, pulling out Buck's wallet. He'd already taken the cash out of the wallet but hadn't bothered with the credit card, being fairly certain that Buck wasn't the kind of guy that had any credit to his name.

"Yeah, it's a wooden house on Benhill. Don't know the exact address, but it's only a few blocks from your house."

Joe brought the car to a halt, and he and Bernard helped Jackie into the emergency room, where he'd wait for another three hours, clutching the extra spray bottle of Narcan that Joe gave him and fingering the baggie of street oxys in his pocket.

24

Roland Hines didn't want to leave 3Make when he was 60. He was healthy, both mentally and physically, and brewing with ideas. But the ideas didn't jibe with the initial financial backers. Roland had built the company based on his ability to see what was going to be the most important developments ahead for the 3D printing industry. While everyone else was focusing on the hardware side of things, Roland thought the real revolution was in the materials used for manufacturing.

Despite Roland's expertise, the initial investors in 3Make were enamored by machines. They came from the computer numerical control (CNC) world, where the developments were driven by better hardware. When the initial investors first saw a 3D printing machine in action, they were gobsmacked. Roland tried to explain the market landscape and the fact that there were now at least a dozen manufacturers worldwide that could build decent machines. Building a good machine, Roland told them, would soon be as easy as making a smart washing machine. But he was not fully believed; not by the investors, the Board, or the guy who was installed as CEO.

So, Roland took his buyout and left, completely, until the new venture capital firm TripleDouble paid off 3Make's debt and their chief operative, Bernard Jamal, came to visit Roland and pick his brain. By that time, Roland had been "retired" for a couple of years. He had installed a 3D printer in the basement of his house that he could use to experiment, but nobody in 3Make management at that time paid much attention to what he was doing.

When Roland laid out his vision to Bernard, the guy kept nodding and taking notes. Listening. What a concept, thought Roland, a VC guy who wants to know more about what the founder of the business he's largely funding is thinking. Roland held back no punches, but Bernard didn't flinch. He kept asking the kind of questions that Roland had hoped to receive over the last five years at 3Make, but never came close to hearing. Bernard didn't want any pie-in-the-sky stuff. He was focused in the same way as Roland: He wanted to know the rewards and risks, the competition's advantages and disadvantages, and the hardcore nuts and bolts of how to get to their goal before anybody else who might have similar plans.

Roland was ready for Bernard's visit. He didn't have any illusions about starting up another company or going back to work full time, but he thought he might be able to get a lucrative consulting gig out of the meeting. He built an engineering plan based on a single foundation: developing new designs and materials that could produce parts and assemblies with characteristics never seen before.

Roland believed there was vast potential for plastic materials that delivered all the benefits of metal, but were more flexible, malleable and durable. Plastics with the elasticity of rubber, but with unprecedented long-term performance. Hybrids that merged the best characteristics of different materials. New materials would give engineers the ability to consolidate multiple parts into single part assemblies that were lighter weight and more efficient. Roland took pride in developing the plan and finally being able to present it to someone who might help it come to fruition. To his credit, Bernard accepted the plan in full.

The challenge was implementation, but Roland had a plan for that too. He still had connections throughout the industry; people who respected what he had done and his ideas for what the future would hold. What initial investors in 3Make didn't grasp, some others did. Roland and his believers lacked only one thing: someone with money to back his plan.

Once Roland was assured he had the backing of TripleDouble, he recruited an engineering team that could fulfill his vision. It was a team culled from around the world, taking in engineers who had become frustrated by their employer's pace of development, their lack of recognition about what drives the market, their under-market-value wages, or the fact that as university researchers they couldn't profit from their work in the way they wanted. Roland, thought to be no more than a very smart engineer, showed considerable skill as a recruiter, drilling down to the base needs of recruits: the desire for respect, the ability to earn the type of money that could buy some dreams, making these engineers feel like they were part of an effort that could change mainstream engineering and manufacturing.

As the team was brought together and Roland kept requesting increased resources, Bernard didn't balk at anything. It was as if Roland had a personal genie, granting him his every wish, business- and engineering-wise. Roland didn't want to go back to work as a full-time executive—every minute he spent in a meeting room was like a piece of skin being peeled away from his body—and Bernard protected him from that. When Roland was able to pry Bill Christenson, his former top engineer, from a competitor that was foolishly courting the home 3D printing market, he felt as if he had all the elements in place to step away almost completely.

But in recent months, Roland had become less assured about the direction of the company and his role in it. Nothing had changed with Bernard and TripleDouble. Surprisingly, the main issues that Roland had were with Bill Christenson, the person he had hand-picked to fulfill his engineering vision.

Roland always knew that Bill had an ego, and rightfully so to a certain extent. He was a smart and practical engineer, with a mind that could take in a vast amount of information, process it quickly, and come up with a solution. He was a rational guy who didn't mind a bit of a gamble if it made engineering sense. But he also liked praise and reinforcement. When they worked together, Roland fed him what he needed. But Bill was older now, with a younger second wife and a mortgage on a huge McMansion. He had a new level of ambition that Roland had not seen before. An avaricious ambition, Roland thought.

25

Tony, Charlaine and Jacey sat at an oval table in the conference room of DII, located in an industrial area just east of Carroll Park and west of M&T Bank Stadium. The building was a one-story, 4,000-square foot open space that used to house a machine shop that supplied tooling for Continental Can. Everybody at DII thought Tony chose the building because it was cheap, and that might have been part of the reason. But Tony had other, more pressing reasons. The building was convenient for hopping on main arteries in all directions and it was in a discreet location within an industrial park. It was also a blank canvas.

The building looked abandoned from the outside, just like Tony wanted it to look. It was hideously ugly, with boarded up windows and bricks covered in thick soot. Inside, there was a building inside a building; a separate infrastructure that enabled a team of builders to completely revamp all the electrical, mechanical and HVAC systems. All the computers had updated operating systems and the latest hardware. Fiber cable ran throughout the building and the Wi-Fi signals were strong and secure.

The three people meeting in the office were facing a rare situation: They all had failed in some way or another in their engagement with the mysterious client. Tony initiated the whole thing by failing to vet the client. Jacey had been unable to track the source of the emails that were sent to engage DII, and Charlaine had been unable to stop the abduction of Bernard Jamal.

But they weren't there to rehash what they did or didn't do. They were there to unravel the mystery of who hired them and why, along with trying to locate Jamal, if he was still alive, and find out the reasons for his abduction, if that's what it was.

"Okay," said Tony. "Let's do the usual and start with what we know. Someone hired us to shadow Prisha Kapoor and find out if she was doing something that runs against the best interests of 3Make. She met with Jamal, whose VC firm TripleDouble provides a big chunk of funding for 3Make. After their meeting, Kapoor and Jamal separate to go to their cars, parked in opposite directions from one another. Jamal is lured into helping a little redhead and is knocked out by a big white guy, dragged into the trunk, and taken away while Charlaine is held at gun point. Is that it?"

"That's about it," said Charlaine. "I found out a lot about Jamal and his VC firm but it didn't shed a lot of new light on our situation. It looked as if the meeting at the Formosa was business-related, as they didn't stay there long and didn't eat. When they left and talked at the corner for a bit, there was no outward sign of affection, so I don't think it's any kind of affair. As for the abductors, it's hard to figure out any connections to 3Make. Why abduct the VC guy who's providing the biggest share of your funding? And, as I said before, the big-ass guy and little Lucy didn't look like professionals, although they did do the job; the first part anyway."

Charlaine and Tony looked at Jacey, who was immersed in her laptop, seemingly not paying attention. But as soon as she realized that she was being prompted, she folded down the screen and rested her fingers on top.

Jacey was 26 years old and had joined the firm after slogging through five years with a gaming start-up that never took hold. She was a short, round woman who drank a six-pack of Mountain Dew a day and liked Club crackers with cheddar cheese spread. Her work wardrobe comprised five versions of the same black dress, accented by a collection of colorful scarves. She wore industrial-strength Wolverine boots all-year round with socks of different hues and designs that came to her knees.

"It's a shitfest for sure," she said. "I'm losing sleep and with my metabolism I can't afford that. I can tell you one thing for certain. This client, or someone in his or her organization, is very sophisticated. I've used every email tracking tool and strategy I know and I still can't find where those emails originated."

"Not to be traitorious, Jace," said Tony, "but do you know anybody who might know something you don't?"

Jacey tried to maintain composure, but Charlaine could see a trace of a grimace. Jacey had talked to Charlaine a few times about what she thought was Tony's lack of respect for her skills and experience.

"No, Tony," she said softly through gritted teeth. "I'm pretty good at this, you know. Better than anyone in my circle and almost everyone outside of it. I mean, it's my life."

"I didn't mean to disparate you, Jace," Tony mumbled softly. "I just want to get to the bottom of this."

"We all do, Tony, we all do," said Charlaine. "We've gone over what we've done, what we know and what we don't know. What's our next move?"

"Okay, here's my suggestion," said Tony, glad to be on firmer ground. "Charlaine, you keep probing on the Jamal side of things, trying to figure out what's what with his abduction. Contact the girlfriend. Try to find out if there is any friction between TripleDouble and 3Make. Sometimes these financial wonks and the companies they invest in make for strange bedfellows. Jacey, keep trying to find out more about 3Make, whether they or anyone in their management has had shady dealings in the past. I'm going to send an email to our mystery client telling them we're resigning the case unless they can shed some light on what they are actually digging for and why they think this Prisha woman needs to be monitored. I'm also thinking that the former 3Make owner, a Roland Hines, would be worth talking to. Maybe he was ousted and has a bone to pick or has some dirt on the new management team. I saw on their website that he is still listed as a Consulting Executive, whatever that is, and he still sits on the Board. Keep me posted on any developments. Agree?"

Charlaine and Jacey shook their heads in the affirmative. Tony placed his hands on the table and pushed himself up from his chair.

"Do we still love one another?"

"Yes, Tony," Charlaine and Jacey replied in sing-song fashion, like good first graders.

26

The Uber driver pulled into the driveway behind the house as Buck had instructed him. His name was Advic and he wore a royal blue turban around the top of his head. A brilliant white smile popped from his smooth, mahogany-colored face.

Happy fucker, thought Buck. *Probably dreaming about planting a bomb in city hall.* There weren't many of these guys around when Buck was growing up, but now they are everywhere.

"Hello, are you Bernard Jamal?" Advic asked, without a hint of irony or suspicion.

"Yes, I am, every day," Buck answered cheerfully. He could end up enjoying this.

"How is your day, sir?"

"Getting better, Advic, getting better."

Buck had decided that his cousin Patrick provided the best option for hanging out and plotting his next move. Patrick lived by himself in a basement apartment in Essex. It was one of those neighborhoods with a lot of transients and people didn't ask questions. Buck thought of it as a don't-ask-don't-tell zone. Patrick pretty much had to take Buck in because he owed him a fair sum of money: $450 Buck had advanced him for coke buys when he was flush and Patrick was broke. Buck would rescind some of the debt in exchange for a few weeks of safe lodging in a neighborhood where he wouldn't attract attention.

After the initial rage, Buck felt peaceful, even grateful. Might have been those tokes of Blue Dream before Advic arrived. Buck loved weed, but wished the effects lasted longer. Like everything good, the initial delirious high thinned out over repeated use. Kind of like sex with the same woman.

Sex didn't do much for him these days. He'd just as soon DIY. Less complicated and you can always guarantee the results. But that chick Ashley made him twitch a bit. He'd like to see if the collar matched the cuffs. And she had some of that redhead spunk, the kind he remembered with Maureen McCormick, who went down on him in high school for a nickel bag, wiped her lips afterward and said, "Was it good for you, big boy?" That was only 13 years ago but Buck was fairly certain they don't make them like that anymore. At least not in the places he hung out.

Even hanging out had become a drag for Buck. What could a bar do for him? He didn't particularly like most people, so hanging out with a bunch of them getting hammered wasn't something he sought. If he was in a bar, it was for business. He might have a shot or two, but that was about it. He saved his inebriation for home, wherever it was that week.

He thought the stay at Patrick's crib would satisfy three goals: Most importantly, it would keep him out of sight from anyone looking for him. Secondly, it would give him time to think. Thirdly, it might speed Patrick's debt payment: The last time he spent several nights at his cousin's place the guy seemed anxious to get rid of him. Buck didn't blame him. He recognized that he wasn't the best company. Most people tolerated him because he had good weed and blow, not because he was a good hang. That was fine with Buck; he didn't want a bunch of hangers on like those NBA players: childhood friends who haven't done a thing with their lives taking handouts from the big money earner.

Nobody had done much for Buck growing up, but they felt compelled to give him advice on how he should conduct his life. His older sister, married to that fake minister, said the Lord would take him in. Yeah, well, Lorton prison would take him in too, but it wasn't Buck's idea of a happy place.

His sister told him "I know there's a good man inside of you, and Manuel and the Lord can bring it out in you." Yeah, Manuel. His sister married a religious Rican. What did he know about Buck except for the fucked up shit his sister told him? "He's always been a troubled boy." Buck thought, yeah, I'm troubled because pops beat the shit out of me while you were graduating from high school and Essex Community, getting your beautician's license and marrying a Jesus freak from one of those mega churches, where all those clean-shaven, righteous bastards and their uptight wives sway to shitty music that sounds like folk singers on ludes.

His sister was always talking about heaven, but Buck didn't believe in that either. He thought there was only life and death. Only idiots thought they were going to be saved and go to heaven, sitting around with the Lord shooting the shit. All because they go to church and praise His name. If the Lord provides, how come so many of those Jesus fuckers are so poor? At least the Black boys dealing on the street know that they're doing the job for which they're best qualified and that the short term is the only term in life. Do it today or regret it later is what Buck thought. If that made him no good, so be it. He didn't choose life, it chose him and gave him an asshole father and a mother who didn't give a shit about how much he was beaten. A mother who told him he was worthless in colorful terms that reside in Buck's brain like a tumor waiting to receive a nice dollop of cancer.

So, it was like the tattoo Buck had imprinted on his left bicep: *Expect Nothing*. That's how he lived his life. Expect nothing and you're never disappointed. Buck wasn't disappointed in Jackie because he had no expectations for him. Jackie was just another person passing through his life and fucking up in the process. *Join the club, Jackie, but know if I see you again, you better take cover as best you can with your big fuckin' ass.*

Advic pulled up to the curb in front of Patrick's place, a row house that was home for a makeshift family of a mother, daughter, grandson and 25-year-old layabout son. Patrick didn't pay much for his one-room basement abode, with the toilet out in the open, a toaster oven and small fridge, and a tiny shower with a moldy wraparound curtain, but it brought in some cash that the family needed.

"Here you are Mr. Jamal. Have a very nice day," said Advic, his teeth gleaming.

Buck picked up his backpack, with all of his current possessions, and opened the back door of the Hyundai.

"You too, Advic. Stay away from city hall."

27

"Do you believe him?" Joe asked Bernard after they dropped Jackie off in the emergency room, promising to return once he was treated. The rough plan was to drive back to Joe's house and leave the Town Car where they had discovered it, but without the keys inside. Then they'd hop in Joe's car and drive around his neighborhood seeing if they might be able to locate Jackie's partner in crime. The next stop would be Canton to try and recover Bernard's car and retrieve a second cell phone that he kept in the glove compartment of the Lexus. Bernard never thought he was tied to his phone, but he felt incomplete without it, or maybe it was the lack of a wallet with his identification and credit cards that was creating the insecurity.

"I don't think he has any motive to lie at this point," Bernard replied, "and if he is lying, he's damn good at it; like professional-level. Maybe I'm Mr. Softee, but I think the guy is basically good. I'd like to see if I can help him."

"You a better man than me, Doc. If he smacked me on the noggin' and stuffed me into an automobile trunk, I'd think of a different fate for his big pale ass. What you gonna do, hire him to be your bodyguard or valet?"

"I don't know. Get him help first. Find out what he can do. You heard him speak. He has a brain on him. That could be me if I wasn't lucky enough to stay healthy when I was playing ball and didn't have the people who helped me navigate college. I did some, shall we say, marginal things, in college that could have backfired."

Joe shook his head.

"You didn't do no abductions, Blood. That's what they call a bridge too far."

"Maybe I can be a bridge over troubled waters, Joe."

"Just make sure that bridge has some strong girders, 'cause you'll need them to carry that weight."

Joe eased the Town Car into the spot where they'd found it and locked it, putting the keys in his pocket. The two men crossed the street, got into Joe's car and took a drive around the neighborhood, looking at the buildings on Benhill Avenue. One house, a two-story wood-framed structure with a cinderblock foundation, looked promising based on Jackie's description. Joe stopped the car a block away and they started to walk toward the house when a white man who looked to be Joe's age stepped out on his stoop and yelled at them.

"Hey, you two! You livin' in that shack?"

Joe tilted his head and looked over the guy from head to toe.

"No, man, I live a few blocks away on Ceddox Street. I'm looking for somebody that might have been living in that house."

"Used to be a young white dude livin' there for a while, but he left a few weeks ago. I'm thinking someone else moved in 'cause I've heard a generator runnin' sometimes at night. I think the summabitch was stealing electric from me while I've been working during the day. Mind if I come with?"

"No, I don't mind," said Joe, "but we're doing what they call 'exercising caution'. We think a guy at this address might have tried to abduct my young friend here."

"Why'd he want to do that? You famous or rich? Play for the Ravens?"

Bernard shook his head. If you were a well-dressed, big Black male in Baltimore, you were likely tabbed as an athlete by older white dudes. They think it's the only way a Black man can succeed in Baltimore, other than politics or drug dealing.

"Neither, man. I don't know why they chose me. That's what we're trying to find out."

The old man pointed at Joe.

"You some kind of investigator or whatchacallit, bounty hunter? Look kinda old for either one, if you don't mind my saying."

"Don't mind you saying, but you should look in the mirror sometime. You no spring chicken. I'm neither one. Just trying to help out the Doc here."

"So you're a doctor? No wonder. They probably wanted you to get drugs for them. Most of the boys under 30 in this here neighborhood are on somethin' or other. Oxy or heroin." He pronounced it *hair-ron*.

"He's no medical doctor, man," said Joe, getting frustrated with the old dude's thickness. "He don't look like Doctor J to you?"

"One of those TV docs used to be on Oprah?"

"No again," said Joe, shaking his head. "Now let's check out the house before whoever is in there gets away while we flap our gums."

"Well, there's been a big pimp-type car—no offense—parked out back, but it ain't there no more."

"That's probably the place then," said Joe. "But again, exercise caution, that boy is armed and dangerous, as they say."

"Who's they?"

"Forget it," said Bernard, now joining Joe in frustration but thinking that the old white man could be useful. "Hey, you mind knocking on the back door while we hide around the side? The guy would recognize us and he's not, uhh, well disposed toward people of color."

"Yeah, sure, I was going to pay a visit anyway. Summabitch stealing my electric."

"Okay, be careful, hear," said Bernard.

The old man nodded.

"No worries. I used to be in the National Guard and I served in 'Nam."

The man hitched up his canvas work pants, held over his belly by red suspenders, walked up the two wooden steps and knocked loudly on the screen door. When no one answered, he pulled open the screen door and pounded on the aluminum back door. Still no answer, so he started calling out "Hey, neighbor" loud enough to wake up the neighborhood dogs two blocks away. Still no answer, so the old man tried the door knob. The door opened with a creak. He peered inside and seeing nothing, opened the door a bit wider and stuck his head inside.

"Looks empty, boys," he shouted to Joe and Bernard, who'd rounded the corner and stood at the bottom of the steps. "Since youse got the weapons, maybe you should go before me. Smells like they been smoking that wacky weed."

Joe and Bernard pulled their revolvers, brushed the old man aside and went inside, where there was a large living area with a kitchen in the back. A door before the kitchen area was left open and revealed a small, stinking bathroom. There was a staircase leading to the second floor where the bedrooms were probably situated, but the wooden steps were rotted and split in places. No way anybody the size of Jackie or Buck could have gotten up those steps.

"Looks like they hightailed it," said the white man.

"Well, one of them did, anyway," muttered Bernard.

"If you catch that summabitch, let me know. I want my electric money back."

"Yeah, sure," said Bernard, knowing that was the least of his concerns.

Joe and Bernard got back in the car and made the 25-minute drive over the Hanover Street bridge through Locus Point and north on S. Clinton Street into Canton. During the course of the ride, the events before he was knocked out started to come into focus for Bernard. They drove a few blocks from the square and found the car parked where it was left early yesterday evening. Bernard had a spare set of keys secured with a magnet inside the back passenger-side wheel well. He unlocked the door while Joe sat in his car with the engine idling.

"Well, Joe, I'd say you're off the clock now. I don't know how to thank you, man."

"You can thank me by keeping me on the know about what's happening. Damn, a real live mystery. My man Walter would love it."

"I'll keep you posted Joe, and would you mind keeping an eye on that Town Car? That redneck Buck might just come back and try to claim it again."

"Yeah, I'll do that, Blood. Me and my cousins, Smith & Wesson, will be watchin'."

28

After retrieving his phone from the Lexus, Bernard limped a few blocks to a coffee shop and ordered an extra-large skinny latte and a toasted English muffin with honey. He should have been hungrier, but food didn't interest him at the moment. He was using the coffee and muffin break to figure out his approach with Roland.

He thought it was best to assume that Roland didn't know anything about Prisha's concerns or why Bernard would be an abduction target. The latter could have been as simple as Jackie said it was: An ill-conceived plan that went wrong. But Bernard kept getting back to the fact that the plan didn't go wrong by much. If he hadn't woken up during the car ride back to the house or hadn't hit Jackie on his bum knee, Bernard might have been holding today's issue of the *Sun* in a video that Jackie or Buck would have sent to TripleDouble along with a request for a couple of million in ransom money.

Bernard unconsciously touched his left temple and winced. He should probably get it looked at. The ankle too. Bernard was a physical person, on and off the court, and always had a bruise or twinge somewhere from trying to carry too much at one time, attempting to open a door when his hands were full, or not using the proper lifting technique. He was often preoccupied and bumped into furniture and walls throughout his house. On the court he didn't shy away from banging inside and sacrificing his body for the sake of a rebound or a drive to the basket. Despite his sometimes carelessness with his body, however, he'd never taken a serious hit to the head. Nor had he ever passed out.

OK, Bernard, compartmentalize. Bring yourself back to the here and now. Concentrate on Roland.

Bernard liked Roland. He thought he was incredibly bright, and unlike some other engineers at 3Make, he was articulate, able to order his thoughts and express them in a way that non-technical folks could understand. Bernard had shown Summers, the best marketing mind he knew, the plan that Roland had developed for 3Make. Summers was impressed. He said what Bernard thought when he first read through the plan: That Roland could have taken it to almost any VC company in the country and they would have coughed up millions on the spot. Bernard felt he was fortunate to have seen it first.

But Bernard didn't want his admiration for Roland's mind to cloud his judgment about his character. There are people out there, Bernard knew, fully capable of putting on a show of fealty to an organization while scheming behind the backs of the Board and fellow executives. He didn't think that was going on with Roland, but he couldn't rule out the possibility. In Bernard's position, one had to see all the contingencies: There was too much money on the table to don the rose-colored glasses.

When Bernard was finished with the muffin, he took the empty plate to a basket on the side of the counter and walked back to the car with his coffee. He thought about going to the office to make the call to Roland, but he didn't want people to see him in his current state, lump on the side of his head, limping on his swollen ankle, dirty clothes, unkempt hair, and stubbly beard. His house was only a few minutes away, but he didn't want to go there either. He wanted to call Roland while everything was fresh in his mind.

He opened the car door, sat in the driver's seat, pulled out his second phone and pressed the number for Roland, hearing it ring on the other end. Roland answered on the third ring, sounding as if he'd been awakened.

"Hullo, Bern. What's up?"

"Sorry to disturb you, Roland. Want me to call back later?"

"Nah, I'm good. I was up late last night fooling around with my VR rig. I think I could be on to something."

Bernard knew that Roland was always experimenting. The latest was trying to optimize software to reduce latency for a VR headset that was not much bigger than a pair of reading glasses. Right now he was in that trap familiar to VR software developers, where the latency is at a level that causes a version of motion sickness, with the mind not quite convinced that the environment is real.

"Good to hear. Keep us posted on how it develops. Do you mind switching your brain over to 3Make?"

"Sure, that's what I'm here for. How can I help?"

"I'm not sure you can, but I wanted to run some strange recent happenings by you."

"I'm the king of strange. What's up?"

"I had a meeting with Prisha yesterday in private and she's concerned about the secretive nature of the nightshift. She tried to go into that part of the lab and they wouldn't let her enter."

"Who's they?"

"A guy she didn't know working in the lab. He left her outside the locked door and supposedly called Bill, who told him that she wasn't allowed to enter. When Prisha asked Bill about it the next day she said he basically brushed her off."

"I don't know why he would do that. There's nothing secretive about the work they're doing as far as I know."

"Yeah, that was our understanding too. Is there any reason why Bill would not want Prisha to see what was going on in that part of the lab?"

"No reason that I can see. He told me that Prisha was concerned about him going over budget, but that's no cause for secrecy. I gotta say that Bill and I haven't been too close over the last six months or so. My take is that Bill thinks the plan is moving too slowly, although he hasn't said that directly to me."

"Do you think it's moving too slowly?"

"No, it's going exactly how I expected. The material developments we're working on are complex. There's a reason other companies aren't invested in it like we are. Beyond the development process itself, there's all the coordination among developers around the world that has to be managed. You guys aren't pressuring Bill, are you?"

"No, not at all. We believe in the plan and if you think that it's going according to schedule, that's good enough for us."

"Okay. I thought as much. You've always been a straight shooter."

"Any suggestions on how to handle the situation?"

"Yeah. Let me start by talking with Bill. It's his operation. Maybe there's something going on that he's not aware of. We're growing so fast that there could be some guys who are not on the right track. That's no knock on Bill. Shit happens when you're juggling a lot of projects. There also might be some things Bill doesn't want other managers to know about just yet because they don't understand the R&D process and might make false assumptions."

"Okay, report back to me after you talk with Bill. Oh, and there are a couple of other things." Bernard said it casually, as if he was mentioning the weather.

"Lay them on me."

"Prisha is certain she saw Spencer Ohtari in the 3Make parking lot the same night that she was refused admittance to the nightshift lab."

Roland let out a low, long whistle.

"Spencer Ohtari? What would that asswipe be doing at 3Make?"

"Exactly. What do you know about Ohtari? I heard he didn't leave Sintology on his own accord. You know what happened?"

"I know a little. A guy who handled material acquisition for Sintology was in cahoots with Ohtari for a while until the guy accepted Jesus Christ as his savior. He told his wife and the CEO of Sintology at the time, Craig Worthington, about what was going on."

"How did you find out?"

"Worthington and I used to talk. I don't like most CEO types, but Worthington was a good dude. We'd meet at a bar about every other month and shoot the shit. He'd complain about his engineers and I'd complain about the marketing peeps. Worthington was supposed to be under non-disclosure, but you know how that works: You don't want a guy like Ohtari working in the industry, even if he gets a job with a competitor. Worthington was getting ready to retire and I think he wanted to get this off his chest, especially because he knew Ohtari would likely apply for a position at 3Make, which he did, by the way. You know there's a lot of talk about the ruthlessness of people in business, but I've found that the people in the 3D printing world value honesty a lot more than in other areas of technology. They know a few bad apples at the executive level can screw up things for the entire industry, especially from an investor's standpoint."

"Did Worthington say what Ohtari was doing or suspected of doing?"

"No suspected—he did it. Worthington swore me to secrecy, but I'm going to trust you. Craig told me Ohtari was connecting the acquisition guy with Chinese and Russian sources for materials. The acquisition guy was going along with Ohtari's scheme until he started getting reports from the field that the materials weren't performing up to spec. That was about the time the acquisition guy started courting the Lord and told his wife what was going on. She threatened divorce if he didn't report it to Worthington. Some guys would have welcomed the prospect of a divorce from that woman, but as I said, this guy was under divine influence."

"This just keeps getting richer and richer. And that's not everything."

"Dare I ask what else?"

"Prisha talked to me about her concerns at a bar in Canton. Afterwards, to make a long story short, I was smacked on the head, thrown into the trunk of a Lincoln Town Car, and abducted by two guys. I escaped and early this morning me and an old guy who helped me found one of the guys behind the scheme, OD'd in the driver's seat of the Lincoln but still alive. He's in the hospital now being treated. He says he has no connection to 3Make or anybody else in the 3D printing business."

"Christ on a cracker! What the hell would they want with you? Do you believe the abductor?"

"Yeah, he has no reason to lie, but I'm going to pick his brain a little more when he gets out of the hospital. I'm going to keep investigating the abduction on my end, but do me a favor: Don't mention that part of it to anyone else, especially not Bill. Probably best not to mention the Ohtari sighting at this point either."

"Roger that. Have you thought about going to the cops?"

"Sure, I did. But I don't want anything to get out about this. I don't want to create a circus around TripleDouble or 3Make."

"Okay, I trust you on that and will keep quiet about Ohtari and the abduction attempt. Meanwhile, I'll think of an approach that might draw something out of Bill. This is a far piece from business as usual."

"You got that right, brother. Let's keep in touch."

"You got it, captain."

29

Charlaine pulled up near the front of Jamal's house on N. Collington and verified the address she'd written down. It was a modest house for a guy in Jamal's position. She knew from the *Sun* article that his live-in partner had an executive-level job at a PR firm so was probably bringing home big bucks herself. What Charlaine didn't know was that Jamal and his partner Kensey also owned three other houses on the block; one for Bernard's mother and sister, another for Kensey's aunt, and a third next door that would allow them to expand their residence.

Charlaine was approaching the front door when a well-dressed white woman stepped out on the stoop and closed the door behind her. Charlaine flashed her best smile and called out in a neighborly voice.

"Good morning! Kensey Mathers?"

The woman looked at Charlaine with a mix of curiosity and caution.

"Yes, I'm Kensey, but I'm in a rush and don't have time to talk."

"Well, it'll only take a minute and I guarantee you'll be interested. Have you talked to Bernard since last night?"

Kensey was taking the car keys out of her pocketbook. She stopped dead and looked up.

"Why do you want to know?"

"I'm a private investigator, Miss Mathers. I was in Canton last night on another matter and saw your husband get knocked out and thrown into the trunk of a Lincoln Town Car. I tried to help, but a little bit...a little redheaded woman who was with the guy that knocked your Bernard out pulled a gun on my aaa...on me and told me to hold still. They hopped in the car and drove away. I wanted to see if you'd heard from him. If he's safe, I'd like contact him to tell him what I know. If he's missing, I can help find him."

Kensey clutched the car keys to keep her hands from shaking and dropped back on defense.

"Why didn't you call the cops? And why should I trust you?"

"It was a rather sensitive situation and I didn't think the police would be much help to your man."

"You sound like Bernard. Sorry, I'm not stereotyping here, just saying. Can you show me a license or something?"

Charlaine pulled a laminated private detective license with her picture on it out of her wallet and passed it over to Kensey.

Kensey took the license in her shaky hand, examined it for a few seconds, and handed it back.

"Sorry for the third degree, but this is coming too fast. Bernard called me early this morning. He was safe in a house in Curtis Bay with an old man who took him in. They were going to do a neighborhood search and then go back to Canton to get Bernard's car. I'm thinking he has his backup phone by now, so I'll call him and see if he wants to talk with you. Then I need to get going to an interview."

Kensey backed up a few steps from Charlaine, dug out a phone from her pocketbook and called Bernard, who answered on the first ring. Charlaine could hear parts of Kensey's low voice telling Bernard what was happening, and saw her nodding when he responded. She disengaged from the call and put the phone back in her pocketbook.

"He says he has a few things to do, like getting cleaned up, but he'll meet you in two hours. Do you know Vikki's Deli in the Broadway Market?"

"I've never been there, but I'm sure I can find it. I'll be about ready for lunch by that time anyway. Thank you, and good luck with your interview."

"Thanks, I'll need it after the night and morning I've had. I feel like a wreck. Good luck getting to the bottom of this mess."

"You don't look like a wreck, girl; you can take that to the bank. We'll get to the bottom of this, I guarantee you, Miss Mathers."

"Call me Kensey, please. Miss Mathers is my aunt."

30

Spencer Ohtari picked up his phone and saw it was a call from a private number. Probably Mikhail. Mikhail was Spencer's most reliable ally and a solid guy. It didn't take much to motivate him: Suffuse him with cash and he'll perform reliably. He'd done it before, setting up the supply chain for cheap materials while Spencer was at Sintology. Spencer would have been sitting on top of the world now at Sintology, raking in record profits and getting huge annual raises from the Board if it wasn't for that acquisition guy who found the Lord. Spencer answered the call without saying hello or mentioning Mikhail's name.

"There's some trouble," said Mikhail. He had a neutral voice that could have come from anywhere. Spencer had only met him face-to-face once, around 10 years ago. Just like his voice, his looks held no clue to his identity. He looked like a generic, white engineer: Average height and weight; lanky dirty-blond hair; khakis, plain polo shirt, off-brand sneakers.

"What sort?"

"Jamal called Roland this morning and my guy listened in on the tap. Jamal met with Prisha last night and she told him that she tried to get into the nightshift lab, but they wouldn't let her in. She talked to Christenson about it and he didn't satisfy her curiosity. So she went to Jamal and told him everything that bothered her."

"Did that PI agency we hire say anything about the meeting?"

"No. But they are suspicious about why we're having them follow Prisha. They sent an email a half-hour ago demanding to know who we are and why we want them to follow her. They threatened to resign if we didn't give them more information."

Mikhail recited the information in a deadpan voice, but Spencer could hear a hint of disgust.

"What did you tell them?"

"I told them they'd have to give back the retainer. I thought if they saw that money go away, they'd think twice. But, they didn't take the bait. So I told them they were fired and I'd leak out to the community how incompetent they are."

"How'd they respond?"

"Son of a bitch just replied 'fine'."

"Cheeky bastards. You think they'll leave us alone?"

"Yeah, no money, no motivation to continue. I'm not worried about them. But there's something else."

"Spit it out, man."

"Prisha told Jamal that she saw you in the 3Make parking lot after hours, the same night she tried to enter the lab, and Jamal told Roland. Showing up at 3Make isn't a smart move, Spencer."

Spencer let out a stream of air over the phone, but his voice stayed even.

"I don't need any remonstrations from you, Mikhail. I thought it was safe since it was dark and after hours. I can smooth that over if I have to. I still have friends in the industry and it's not against the law to visit them."

"No, it isn't, but that's a secure facility and it was after hours. Is there someone who could vouch for you?"

"Well, Barrett worked at Sintology, so I could say I was visiting him as a friend if pressed on it. But, I have no need to say anything at this point. I'm a private citizen visiting a friend."

"I guess that'll have to be okay for now. But there's something else. Roland told Jamal why you left Sintology."

Spencer exhaled again, this time with more force. His voice raised half an octave.

"I could sue that son of a bitch!"

"You could, but you'd have to say how you found out. Couldn't say you heard it on a phone tap."

"No, of course not. I always suspected there would be a leak. Did Roland tell Jamal who told him about my leaving? Was it that fucking acquisition guy, DeAngelo?"

"No, it was Worthington."

"Of course it was. Those old fuckers in this industry are like a bunch of gossipy women. Damn, I wish I could sue his balls off."

"Worthington's dead now, so that won't work."

"I should have gotten rid of DeAngelo when I had the chance. He's the one who fucked everything up."

"Water under the bridge. We can still arrange for him to be, uhh, favorably disposed, if we need to."

"No, let's hold tight for now and track their next move. Everything is conjecture on their part at this stage."

"But the conjecture is getting a little close for comfort."

"Okay, I'll make sure that Barrett and Chen stay the course and keep their mouths shut. No reason to blow anything up. We're almost there. Just a few more months and it'll be like printing money."

"Glad you think it's that easy. And there's one more thing."

"Jesus, are you shitting me?"

Ohtari thought he heard a quiet sigh on the other end of the line.

"Jamal told Roland that after he met with Prisha he was knocked out, thrown into the trunk of a car, and taken to a place called Curtis Bay, but he escaped when the abductor guy opened the trunk."

"Unbelievable! This just keeps getting more bizarre. What would someone want with Jamal?"

"That's exactly what Roland asked him. Jamal later found the guy who knocked him out and put him in the car trunk. He told Jamal that he and another guy kidnapped him to get a ransom from TripleDouble."

"Jesus, if this was a TV show, nobody'd believe it."

"Yeah, too bad for us it isn't fiction."

Mikhail hung up the phone and walked out onto his deck overlooking the Intracoastal Waterway in Jacksonville Beach, Florida. Nobody knew he was there, in the condo he'd owned for the last 10 years.

He didn't like Ohtari's reaction to the information he gave him. He acted cool, but even over the phone Mikhail could hear the turmoil inside. It was a skill of his: detecting fear, even a small dose of it, and even over the phone. In Mikhail's considerable experience, fear causes irrationality, and irrationality can ruin an operation.

Ohtari wanted to sound optimistic when he was saying they are so close. That it was like printing money. Mikhail knew better. There were still so many loose ends. Ohtari was trying to assure Mikhail, as if he was a Board member for one of those tech companies.

Mikhail thought the source of most of his concerns was not anyone associated with 3Make, but Ohtari. Ohtari had the ego to think he was the main cog in this operation, and Mikhail didn't disabuse him of that notion as long as everything was going okay. The 3D printing part was vital to the project, but the most important component was the battery technology coming out of Fujian province in China. The design and additive manufacturing of the shell with a completely new material was no doubt groundbreaking, but would be nothing without the battery. The 3D printing was innovation, the battery was a paradigm-shattering invention.

It might be time to make a trip to Baltimore, just to be able to react in real time to new developments. If it was necessary to make changes to the team, Mikhail would need to be there to direct the operation. Or maybe take hands-on measures.

31

"What's up, Tiger?"

Charlaine had just gotten into her car after talking with Kensey Mathers when Tony called.

"We just had an exchange with our former employer. We're off the 3Make case, if there ever was a case."

"That was fast, even for you, Tony. Does that mean I won't get a Fall bonus this year?"

For some reason that he never explained, Tony liked September, and chose it as the month to give out extra pay to his best performers, of which Charlaine was always one. She had tried to figure out what it was about September, but had come up empty handed so far. *So far* being the key phrase. No one hid things from Charlaine for long, something Joy found out the hard way when she tried to throw a surprise birthday party for her partner three years ago. A week before the event, Charlaine called a meeting and laid out all the inconsistencies in Joy's behavior over the last month. Joy, the most stoic of women, broke into tears and confessed her plans. She never again tried to surprise Charlaine.

"We'll survive, Goddess. We tried to pressure the mystery client into telling us who they are and what their intentions might be and they refused to devolve the information. So, we're fired. Terminated. Made redundant. Finito."

"I get the idea, Tony. Jacey have any luck tracing the messages?"

"No, she's tried every trick in the book. Nada. They're 'scarily good' she said. I wish I knew she was scarily good. I don't know about her sometimes. That nose ring bugs me. That's a cootie ring if you ask me."

"She's fine, Tony. Since when did piercings bother you? You had a temp once who had piercings on every visible part of her body."

"Yeah, but she was a temp. Carmelo is gaga over Jacey. Always wanting to visit the office. Like he's suddenly interested in the old man's job. He comes in carrying all these books—Kahlil Gibran and that kind of stuff—acting like he's all deep inside. I'm afraid the next things he's going to want are tats and earrings."

"He might look good with a diamond stud and a tat sleeve. Maybe that skinny Black kid would give him more space on the court."

"Yeah, Carmelo would be a regular Dennis Rodman. Here's the thing, Goddess. I'm not sure I want to let this go. I hate a mystery. Can't read one or even watch on TV."

"Yeah, I know, Tone. What is it you say? 'A mystery is just a drummed up conundrum'?"

"That's right. I love when you quote me accurately. What do you think?"

"I think I'm with you, Boss. I don't like getting a gun pointed at me by a puny redhead. It fucks with my pride. I also don't like seeing a fine Black man hit on the head and thrown into a car trunk, even a roomy one. So, I'm on it like Ed Reed on a rookie wide receiver. And speaking of fine Black men, I'm meeting Mr. Jamal in a couple of hours."

"Do tell."

"I met his girlfriend just now outside their crib. She's a cute one. Played guard for Mercy. Jamal is safe for now. He escaped from those abductors and discovered one a couple of blocks away in the Lincoln, passed out on opioids. Woulda probably died if not for Jamal and an old man who was helping him. Kensey, Jamal's partner, is in a bit of shock. I'm sure she had nothing to do with his abduction."

"Okay, stay on it for now, Godly One, and get back to me after your meeting. One other thing..."

"Yes, Tony, I'll try to get a paying client out of this, if I can."

"How did I ever live without you?"

"You have Lidia. Don't forget that. And you have Jacey. Be good to her, Tony, I think she's a keeper."

"Okay, Miss G. I trust your woman's intuity."

32

Bernard pulled into the diagonal parking space in front of his row house on N. Collington. He was an excellent parallel parker, with an uncanny instinct for cutting just the right angle to back a car into a tight space on the first try. Still, he liked the diagonal parking spaces on his block, which prevented less skillful parkers from messing up his ride.

Pushing through the front door he was hit by the smell of recently brewed coffee. Kensey was a coffee maven, grinding fresh beans every morning and putting them into a percolator that she'd inherited from her aunt, who now lived three doors up from them and was perfectly content with her automatic drip coffee maker that uses pre-measured pods. Kensey liked old, solid appliances that worked. The percolator is nearly 50 years old and has stayed functional with replacement lids and new power supplies over the years.

In the confines of his own home, with his senses coming back to normal, Bernard realized that he stunk. Joe had too much class to mention it, but Bernard smelled like he'd taken a dip in the Inner Harbor. He stripped off his clothes and stuck them in a duffle bag. He'd drop the clothes off at the cleaners on his way to Fells Point to meet the PI woman, Charlaine Pennington. Bernard and Kensey had a small washer/dryer combo in an upstairs closet next to the bathroom, but he didn't have time to launder the dirty clothes and he didn't want the smell to linger. He and Kensey shared a sensitive olfactory sense; nice for fine dining, but not an asset at times when the city smelled like a damp alley cat.

Bernard stripped bare and stepped gingerly into the shower stall, putting the bulk of his weight on his healthy ankle. The other ankle was sore and bore colorful swirls of black and blue, but Bernard could still use it if he didn't let it bear his full weight. Joe had done him a huge favor by applying ice to the head and ankle wounds to reduce swelling.

Bernard turned the shower dial to hot, put his head under the spray and let the water slide down the side of his head. He winced when it hit the wound but held still, thinking that the water was providing a healing warmth. After he soaped up and rinsed off, he lingered in the hot water, letting it suffuse his entire body. He thanked himself for buying a hot water heater that supplied twice the capacity normally required for a house his size. He figured he'd need it for future expansion of the house, but didn't realize how nice it was no matter what he planned for the next-door space.

He ran a towel over his hair and studied his face in the mirror. His skin was milk chocolate, supple and smooth. He pumped moisturizer into his palm, rubbed his hands together and massaged his face, careful not to touch the knob on his left temple. He shook his head slightly, wishing he could turn the clock back by a day.

Since before his sophomore year of college, he'd been careful. After his freshman year when he became the second-leading scorer and the top rebounder for UWB, he'd gone a little wild, getting high nearly every night and hanging out in the summer on playgrounds where heroin and coke were being dealt and guns were carried by practically everyone not playing in the pick-up games. Then a week before UWB practice started, Stacy Greer was shot and killed after arguing with a two-bit gangster over a foul in a pickup game on the west side. Stacy was heading into his senior year at UWB after leading the conference in scoring and assists. He was a nice guy in Bernard's eyes, always ready with advice that helped Bernard improve his game: how to overplay lefthanders, the effectiveness of a simple pivot fake in one direction and a fast crossover move in the opposite direction, how to mentally speed up and slow down as required by the situation. But Stacy was a shit-talker, a joyful one like Bernard, but for some the tone and intention didn't matter, especially if it came from a visitor to a player's home court. When the game was over, Stacy gathered up his stuff and was walking away when the bullets went through his back, one of them lodging in his heart. The only mercy was that death came quickly.

After Stacy's killing, Bernard took stock. He got more serious. His father had died from lung cancer when Bernard was a senior in high school, and his mother and sister were working 15-hour days to pay the rent on their 900-square-foot row house in the Greenmount East neighborhood. The life expectancy in that neighborhood was 66 years, compared to 84 years in Roland Park, just five miles away. Bernard knew his mother, 58 at the time, couldn't keep up her work pace too much longer. Arthritis was settling into her joints, requiring her to soak in a tub of hot water for a half-hour or more when she returned home from work at the Dollar store. Other guys could play around with college and on the streets, but not Bernard. He had responsibilities. He didn't give up weed and beer, but he cut back and only partied when he didn't have practice or a game the next day. He got a job the following summer at the Advanced Auto Parts warehouse, unloading freight cars and filling orders during the day and playing ball at night on courts where he knew the other players. He owed it to his mother and sister not to put himself in danger.

There were contingencies associated with his job that Bernard knew well: The stress of making big investments in unproven companies; the long work hours monitoring the businesses TripleDouble invested in; allaying investors' ongoing fears; burnout from the incessant grind; lack of sleep and proper nutrition. Getting struck on the head, thrown into a trunk, and shot at didn't fit the job description. But, he was Black. And he lived in Baltimore.

As he pulled a sock over his tender ankle, Bernard wondered what information Charlaine Pennington might have to offer. He'd googled her and found out a little. Her agency, DII, had a few cases that had made the news: They found a priest in the rural town of Powellville on the Eastern Shore after he left his Baltimore parish with $30,000 of the budget allotted for youth group activities. They provided evidence that helped indict a chiropractor who'd collected insurance money from patients who were already dead. Pennington herself had made the *Sun* when she tracked down a counterfeiter spreading bogus twenties in bodegas and liquor stores in West Baltimore. Bernard thought a Black woman PI must be a rare species, about as rare as a Black former college basketball star turned venture capitalist.

Bernard always liked to be the first one at any meeting. He wasn't when he met Prisha and wished he had been. Maybe he would have seen something at the Formosa that would have tipped him off to his eventual abduction. In this case, he wanted to get to Vikki's Deli early and occupy a stool to see Charlaine Pennington approach. He usually learned something by the way a person entered a room or building, especially if they were not on guard. Often a person would show nervousness or brazenness by the way they walked or their posture. Sometimes they'd be visibly distracted or would do things they wouldn't normally do in public, like pick their nose, make weird facial gestures, or bop around to music from ear pods. It all helped create a composite picture.

He didn't realize that Charlaine had similar habits ingrained into her as a PI. Always get there first. Survey the scene. Look for signs of trouble or suspicious characters. Plan escape routes. She didn't think she necessarily had to do that in a public place such as Broadway Market, but she took precautions because there is always a first time. So she spotted Bernard before he saw her, and he immediately acknowledged her when she waved.

He had a nice walk. Charlaine thought she could immediately recognize someone who'd played basketball in high school or college. Nice long strides. Fluidity in their movements. No favoritism of their right or left side. A little spring to the step. In the best case, exuding something she could only define as sensuality.

Bernard shook her hand, both of their grips firm, but not overbearing.

"Glad to meet you, I think," said Bernard, chuckling a bit.

Charlaine returned a grin and a brief laugh.

"My boss says nobody actually wants to meet someone in our occupation. Especially when they've been on the bad end of the bargain. How are you feeling?"

Bernard briefly touched the bandage he'd applied to his left temple.

"Not bad, considering. Actually I'm glad to meet you, especially given the circumstances. Have you ordered yet?"

"Just an iced tea. What do you recommend?"

"Everything is good here, especially the sandwiches, as long as you're not on a diet. Shrimp salad is always great, but I'm partial to the Baltimore classic, the cloak and dagger."

"Are you stereotyping me?"

Bernard squinted in puzzlement.

"Why would you say that?"

"Private investigator. Cloak and dagger."

"Oh, I get it. Sorry to be slow on the uptake."

"I'll give you a pass this time, considering what you've been through."

"So, you've heard the story?"

"Beyond what I saw for myself, yeah. Your, ahh, woman gave me the brief outline."

"How did she seem to you?"

"A little harried, but understandably. She's a cool customer. I saw her hit two free throws in the state semis to beat Western by one point."

"Did you play?"

"Yeah, for Western. I graduated a couple of years before her. Too bad about the knee injury."

"How'd you know about that?"

"I'm an investigator."

The counter was starting to get a bit crowded, so Bernard suggested they take their food and find a table in another section of the pavilion. When they settled in, he looked around, and seeing they were out of anyone's earshot, got down to business.

"So, how did you come upon my so-called abduction."

"I wouldn't call it so-called. I was on a case that involved following Prisha. When you left the restaurant together, I had to make a decision whether to follow her or you. I figured she was going home, and I was curious as to how you might fit into the scenario. My boss put me in a compromising situation, since I didn't know why I was following Prisha."

"Do you often go into cases not knowing why you're investigating a person?"

"Never. This was the first time. My boss did something he's never done before: Took on a case without knowing the client or why we were investigating. It was a rare misstep. He tried to make the situation right by pressuring the client to reveal him or herself, but they wouldn't do it so he resigned the case and returned the retainer. He didn't like being put in that predicament so he's asking me to investigate. I know the situation sounds unusual, but I can assure you that you are now in good hands."

Bernard rubbed his hands down the side of his face and sighed.

"No offense, Miss Pennington, but what if I don't want your agency involved?"

"That's your choice, but I'd think you'd be curious why someone wanted the chief financial officer of your biggest investment tailed when her work history and record are spotless."

"I am. Very curious. But you don't know why, do you?"

"No, I don't now, but I will."

Bernard raised his eyebrows and laughed.

"I like your confidence. And the fact that your boss offered your services for free."

"He's my boss, but I have a certain level of autonomy. I wanted to follow through on this. At the very least I want to get my hands on that little redhead that set you up and held a gun on my aaa, uhh, person."

"It seems we have some common interests, Miss Pennington. But I always pay for services rendered. Is this when we draw up what those PIs on TV call 'a standard contract'."

"If that's what you want, we'd be happy to oblige. Meanwhile, please refrain from snooping on your own. Best leave these things to professionals."

"I'll do that and there are things you need to know about some suspicious happenings at 3Make. I need to run now, but can I send you an email detailing the situation?"

"Sure, but don't send it from a company email address. In fact, don't talk on a company phone or email from anything connected to a company network. I'll set up a special account for our correspondence. And from now on, call me using this pre programmed phone."

Charlaine pulled an old flip phone from her jacket and handed it to Bernard.

"You think of everything. I'm feeling better already. May I call you Charlaine?"

"You better, 'cause I'm calling you Bernard."

With that, Charlaine wrapped up her cloak and dagger, only a quarter of which she'd eaten. Bernard had polished off the entire shrimp salad sandwich and a bag of chips. He seemed to be getting back to normal.

33

Bill Christenson was entering the parking lot at La Food Marketa when the phone in his pocket buzzed. It was Friday at 1 p.m. and Bill's plan was to have a leisurely meal of crispy fish tacos and a beer or two before changing clothes in his truck and heading out to Pretty Boy Reservoir, where he would go bass fishing for the first time this spring. His flat-bed boat with an electric motor was on the trailer behind his Ford F-150 XL truck. He had serviced the boat the previous weekend and everything was ready to go.

Bill pulled the phone from his pocket and saw it was Roland. He cursed silently. Over the last several months he'd become increasingly annoyed at Roland, going so far as to inquire about other head engineering jobs. He had all the qualifications, but thought that he was meeting with skepticism as some people in the 3D printing industry thought of him as "Roland's Guy," an appellation that suggested he was an acolyte, someone without his own views or unique skills. It didn't bother him so much while he was happy at 3Make, but he was becoming increasingly dissatisfied with his lack of influence over policy decisions.

Over the years, Bill had built a vision for 3Make that differed from Roland's, but he couldn't escape the hold that his once-manager had over the Board. Bill knew the importance of materials and in the last year he'd overseen the development of a new hybrid material that can conduct electricity, giving designers the ability to integrate printed circuit boards and electrical conductivity directly into a part or assembly.

But Bill had other ideas that could establish an industry leadership role for 3Make. He had a vision of a simpler form of design software, untethered from the limitations of CAD, which required years of training and could not always yield designs that were optimized for 3D printing. He also wanted to make 3D printing, or additive manufacturing as it was sometimes called, a fully automated process, from design to part building to cleanup without the need for human intervention.

In his better moments Bill recognized that his frustration wasn't Roland's fault: He was doing what he thought was best for the company. But Bill thought when he was named Chief Engineer that he'd be independent, able to shape the company to his vision. Now, five years into it, he saw that wasn't going to happen. Roland wasn't hands-on, but he wasn't a benign presence either, always asking Bill about project progress; wanting him to share resumés of potential new hires, recommending people he'd worked with in the past; bringing up new projects he wanted the engineering department to pursue, even when Bill was not too keen on his ideas.

Bill's wife Tracey didn't tolerate his complaints too well. She was a human resources consultant and talked a lot about self-fulfillment and creating your own destiny. When Bill confided in her about the issues he was facing at 3Make, she'd listen for about 10 minutes until she became frustrated, commanding him to take action instead of "standing on the sidelines and griping."

Bill had also confided in Chad Odowski, 3Make's CEO, about his frustrations with Roland and the Board looking over his shoulder. Chad wasn't a fount of empathy either. Whenever Bill brought up something that was bothering him, Chad would respond with the equivalent of "you think you have it bad, look at what I have to deal with." Bill didn't think Chad's issues were any greater than his, just of a slightly different nature.

He was probably under a little more pressure, since he had the whole company to manage, but engineering drove the company, and if marketing or sales didn't do their jobs, their people were much easier to replace than elite engineers in the rather proscribed arena of 3D printing.

And now, Prisha was inserting her nose into his business. Roland, Chad, Prisha, Bernard Jamal and the 3Make Board—they just took, took, took. When Bill did something big—like hiring away top engineers from a competitor or leading the team in bringing a new 3D printing material into the market—the glory typically went to Roland. *Functionary* was the word that came to Bill's mind. He was the good soldier, the one who unblinkingly carried out the orders.

He thought about not accepting the call, but Roland would persist in calling him repeatedly over the upcoming hours. So he answered; he hoped with a modicum of pleasantness or at least not transparent resentfulness.

"Heh Roland. How are ya?"

"I'm basking in the sunlight, my friend."

Roland putting on a show, thought Bill. The most contented, positive person on God's green earth.

"Glad to hear, Roland. What do you need?"

"I had a call this morning from Bernard about what might be a little misunderstanding. I thought you could enlighten me."

Yeah, I'll stick a flashlight up your butt, thought Bill.

"I'll try."

Roland told him about Bernard's meeting with Prisha and her concerns. As Bernard requested, he made no mention of the Spencer Ohtari sighting by Prisha or the abduction attempt. When he finished, he posed a variation on the "do you still beat your wife" question.

"Bill, I know you don't have to report to Prisha, but she could make your work life difficult if she had a mind to. You're best advised to be on her good side. So why are you keeping secrets from her?"

Bill's outtake of breath was audible over the phone.

"I didn't think I was, Roland. I just said I wasn't obliged to tell her everything that is happening on the nightshift. I don't know that myself. The whole purpose of the nightshift is for engineers to do independent research. You know that. You set up the thing yourself."

"Yeah, I did, but I don't think the research should be secretive. Prisha has a right to know roughly how the money is being spent, as does the Board and Bernard if it comes to that."

"I guess I'm sick of people looking over my shoulder, including you, Roland. The reason you left was you were tired of the interference."

"No, no, Bill. I didn't leave because I was tired of interference, even though I didn't like it and still don't. I left because their vision of the company's future was fucked. There's a difference. But I can tell you're frustrated. What can I do to help?"

"You can start by trusting me to do my job."

Now it was Roland's turn to expel some air over the phone.

"Okay, okay, Bill. I'll consider that and you can tell me if I'm leaning on you too much. But, for now, we need you to check out the nightshift and find out some more about what's going on there, especially with Barrett and Chen."

"Why Barrett and Chen? You helped vet those guys, Roland. You know how good they are. Why should I step on their toes just because Prisha has issues?"

"I'm singling out Barrett because he worked for Spencer Ohtari at Sintology. And Chen because he's Barrett's friend. Both of those guys are active on the nightshift."

"Other guys worked for Ohtari. Why are you concerned specifically about Barrett?"

"I can't tell you that. If Barrett and Chen check out, we'll move down the line to talk to others doing the nightshift. This is about accommodation, Bill. We all have to do it from time to time. I'm just saying check it out and get back to me. Is that too much to ask?"

He's trapped me again, thought Bill. *If I don't do what he wants I'm going to appear unreasonable.* Bill paused a few seconds before replying. He could hear Tracey saying *have some pride, Bill.*

"Okay, I'll see if I can catch up with them on Monday. I'm taking the rest of the day off for my first bass fishing of the season at Pretty Boy. The wife's at the ocean with her girlfriends so it's shaping up as a boy's weekend. Probably play a round at Piney Branch tomorrow. Anything else?"

"No, nothing else. I appreciate it Bill and hope you hook some big ones."

"No problem, Roland. You have a wonderful day."

Bill ended the call thinking, *why didn't Jamal talk to me directly? It's like Tracey says, "they are either talking with you or talking around you."* Bill had no doubt what category he fell into.

34

Mikhail got the message about Roland's call to Bill Christenson as he was parking his car at Jacksonville International to fly into BWI Airport in Baltimore. The call reinforced Mikhail's decision to be on the scene to iron out the problems that had sprung up around the 3D printing operation. He was kicking himself for trusting Spencer Ohtari. His ego, lack of discipline, need for self-gratification, and insufferable questioning of every detail could derail the most airtight of operations. All he had to do was lay low and stick to the plan. The last thing he should be doing is showing up at 3Make.

The plan required coordination between two teams: The American team, primarily Barrett and Chen, responsible for the design and 3D printing of a non-metal revolver shell, and the Chinese team developing a battery source small enough to fit into the handgrip of the revolver but powerful enough to propel a specialized bullet faster than ever before.

MIT had already come up with two-dimensional polymers that had the strength and durability of steel but with more flexibility and a lot less weight. Chen took that methodology further, adding the ability to use the hybrid material to manufacture the shell with standardized 3D printing systems like those that were now commonplace around the world.

Barrett had come up with the design for the revolver shell, a one-piece part so complex that it could only be manufactured via 3D printing. This was not one of those ghost guns that require assembly and could backfire or break apart at any time. It was a handgun like no other in the history of firearms. Barrett called it The Helix.

Barrett's design didn't require gunpowder or gas as ignition elements. It married a helical chamber with a coilgun, basically a set of cylindrical coils of wire acting as a magnet carrying electric current. The typical problem with a helical chamber is too much vibration from centrifugal force, which would be especially problematic with a lightweight gun. Barrett countered that by having the gun fire two featherweight bullets at a very high velocity in rapid succession. To balance the centrifugal force of one bullet as it goes round, the gun fires another bullet at 180 degrees, which stabilizes the gun. It was similar to how pistons in a multi-cylinder engine are timed so that the forces cancel each other. Once the vibration is taken care of, the magnets inside the helix can progressively accelerate both bullets.

The bullets, made with the same material as the gun, fly at such a velocity that a pair of them can pierce body armor: The first one makes initial penetration and the second one finishes the job, fully piercing the armor and coming out the other side with enough velocity to kill instantly. If the target is an unarmored body, the two bullets will pierce the skin and shatter anything with which they come into contact, including bone, ligaments, muscle, tissue and internal organs. Barrett designed the helical chamber so that it breaks down typical sound waves, acting as a built-in silencer.

Electromagnetic coilguns or railguns have existed for decades, but they've been large and bulky, making a loud sound that can sometimes reach supersonic level. They also require large, unwieldy batteries to power them. The power source is where the Chinese came in.

While the 3D-printed revolver shell married largely existing elements of technologies and research, the battery system for The Helix was a miracle of invention from an elite group of Chinese researchers in the Fujian province. Mikhail tried questioning his Chinese connections to find out more about the breakthrough, but came up empty.

"A new form of lithium-ion?"

"No."

"Vertically aligned carbon nanotubes?"

"No."

"Mesoporous silicon microparticles and carbon nanotubes?"

"No."

"Lithium-sulphur like the Monash University development?"

"No."

"The IBM battery with materials extracted from seawater?"

"No IBM."

"Copper foam substrate?"

"No."

"Sodium-ion?"

"No. And no more speculation."

When the battery prototypes were shipped six months ago, they looked like a flat camera battery. Barrett and Chen were warned not to open them and they complied, not wanting to do anything that would compromise their position with the Chinese contingent. The rechargeable battery was good for 24 shots and fit nicely into the compartment that Barrett had integrated within the gun grip. Under testing in the nightshift lab, the batteries worked as the Chinese team said they would. When Mikhail asked his contact how much they cost to produce and if volume production is possible, he received a terse, but optimistic, reply: "Cheap. Manufacture in millions."

Mikhail was an engineer and understood the technologies behind The Helix. But engineering was not his principal strength. He had worked behind the technological scene for 20 years, the first nine years on a nominally legal basis and the last 11 clandestinely, where the real profits were to be made. He thought of himself as a facilitator, but far from a benign one that coddles multiple parties and uses diplomacy to bring a project to the finish line. He could be kind and thoughtful, but underneath he was a ruthless bulldog who would let nothing stand in his way.

With the design of The Helix completed and early prototypes working largely as expected, it was now time to pull Barrett and Chen out of 3Make and take care of loose ends. The first of these was Bill Christenson. He'd think about Spencer Ohtari, whose connection with Barrett and Chen was once valuable but no longer mattered since both of the engineers were fully in Mikhail's fold. One of Mikhail's specialties was gently nurturing engineers and weaning them away from handlers such as Ohtari. He showed them how eliminating layers of personnel would lead to more money in their wallets. The approach appealed to the engineers' sense of efficiency, their disdain for bureaucracy, and their desire for compensation that would ensure a lifetime of financial independence.

35

The man operating as Brad Davenport this month was sitting in the parking lot of the restaurant watching Bill Christenson on the phone in his truck. He'd begun tailing Christenson this morning, starting out at the 3Make parking lot in Locust Point. He'd had no problem identifying the truck from the description and license tag number Mikhail had given him. Christenson was towing a flat-bed fishing boat; Brad thinking that the guy might go out after work. Instead, he appeared around 12:30 p.m. and drove to a restaurant just over the county line on the northwest side of the city.

Brad had studied up on the locations he was most likely to traverse while following Christenson. He didn't trust navigation systems, relying on his photographic memory and keen sense of direction. Moments after Christenson hung up the phone and started walking toward the restaurant, a call came in from Mikhail. Brad picked up the call and Mikhail started in immediately. The two weren't prone to niceties or social chatting.

"After lunch, he's heading to a place called Pretty Boy to go fishing. Roland just called and asked him to check into what's going on in the nightshift, but he's not going to do that until Monday. I think it's time to make our move. We could probably do it anytime this weekend, but today seems right, especially since the wife is away. Any ideas?"

"Yeah, let me think for a bit and I'll get back to you."

"No need. Call me when you're done."

Brad was looking over a map of Pretty Boy on his phone a minute after he ended the call. He saw there was only one launch ramp on the reservoir, which would work to Brad's advantage. Mikhail would probably want him to do this as simply as possible, but Brad had ideas of his own. He did a search for the best fishing spots on the reservoir and struck gold on a website that had a map of the hot areas for bass this time of year. The best spot was in a cove about a half mile from the boat launch. There were less-attractive spots on the map farther away from the launch site.

Brad did a search for nearby sporting goods stores and saw there was a Dick's in Cockeysville, right off an I83 exit on the way to Pretty Boy. He'd have to work fast, but he thought he had a good plan. He started the Rav 4 SUV that he'd picked up from one of Mikhail's contacts and within 15 minutes he was striding into Dick's. He saw the racks holding the kayaks upright and looked at a blue and green, sit-inside 12-footer, with a weight capacity of 300 pounds. Brad was 5'10" and weighed 175 pounds, so it would work with the extra equipment he needed. He lifted the 55-pound kayak, placed it in the large rolling cart he'd picked up in the entryway, and found a decent paddle that felt solid in his hands. He looked around until he found a kayak transport kit with a pair of soft roof rack bars and bungee cords to secure the bow and stern. He picked up a few more small bungee cords, a pair of binoculars, an all-purpose tarp, and a large sponge. Fortunately, the store was understaffed at this time of day and nobody asked to help him. He took his cart to an open register and within 15 minutes he was out of the store. Once outside, he secured the kayak to the top of the Toyota and made the 25 minute drive to the boat ramp.

It had been just over an hour since he left the restaurant parking lot, so Brad figured Christenson was probably finishing lunch and would be arriving in about 40 minutes. He looked around and was relieved to find nobody on the boat ramp or within viewing distance on the reservoir. He took the kayak down from the roof of the Rav 4, opened the tailgate and lifted up a stiff army blanket. Under it was a trunk that Brad had picked up early this morning after he had arrived at BWI. In it was a lightweight Ruger M77 Mark 2 rifle with a long-range scope, a Colt Python handgun, ammunition, and a Victorinox Hunter Pro folding knife. Both guns were equipped with silencers.

He put the knife in his front pants pocket, loaded the two guns, and placed the rifle inside the kayak and the revolver under the stretch cords in front of the boat's cockpit. He retrieved the bungee cords, sponge, binoculars and tarp from the back of the SUV and placed them in the storage space behind the cockpit of the kayak. After pulling on a pair of gloves, he carried the boat and paddle to the edge of the launching ramp, climbed in, and slid into the water.

Brad loved the feeling of the first gliding of the kayak on the water after launching from shore. He felt weightless and free, which never failed to delight him. The water was clear and cold; Brad had read on one of the websites that it was around 63 degrees. It was mostly sunny, with an array of fluffy cumulus clouds casting shimmering white reflections on the water surface. He got into a paddling rhythm fairly quickly, using the bigger muscles of his chest, back and legs to keep his arms loose and limber.

Brad had been an outdoors person growing up in the Tidewater region of Virginia, where he'd paddled rivers, lakes, streams and salt marshes to fish and hunt. After about 15 minutes of brisk paddling, he guided the kayak into the cove that the website had said was the best spot this time of year for bass.

He immediately saw why this would be a good area for fishing. The water was about 20 feet deep and he could see the outline of tree stumps and the swaying of grass near the bottom. Prime bass habitat. He paddled to the shore, where he grounded the kayak into the reservoir bank below a small wooded hill. There was no one in visible distance of the small cove.

Brad got out of the kayak, taking the rifle and revolver with him. He covered the kayak in leaves and brush and climbed a little way up the hill, setting up on a stump about 20 yards up from the shoreline. All that was left now was to calm himself and wait. All in all, not a bad place to set up shop on a lovely spring afternoon.

36

Bill climbed into the truck and started it up, feeling good after the crispy fish tacos and a bottle of Stella Artois. The weekend had begun and he was looking forward to spending it alone until Tracey's return on Sunday night. They were getting along okay, but there was a quiet tension lingering in the air surrounding them. Bill thought neither of them was to blame: He was internalizing his problems at 3Make and she was tired of listening to him complain. Maybe a weekend apart would lead to a reset, like rebooting a computer after a virus check.

Bill thought briefly about what he'd say to Barrett and Chen, then shook his head in an effort to dislodge the situation from his mind. He'd have plenty of time over the weekend and he didn't want to spoil the serenity of being out on the open water on a beautiful day. Although Bill took pride in his skill as a fisherman, the catching of fish was almost inconsequential. The biggest pleasure quotient was being outdoors and engaging in an activity that always calmed him. To have this type of pristine setting just minutes from his house was a gift.

When he pulled into the parking lot of the loading ramp he saw he was alone except for a small SUV. Probably a kayaker, although he didn't see anyone on the water. *Ahhhh, he'd have paradise to himself.* He got the boat off the trailer and into the water, working quickly from ingrained experience. He started up the small electric engine, which could barely be heard as the boat moved through the water, trailed by a soft, flat wake.

He decided that today he would go to his outermost spots first and work his way back, not spending too much time in any one area unless they were really hitting. He didn't normally keep the fish he caught; he liked bass, but for him this was therapy, not nutrition.

He cruised past one of his favorite spots and was happy to see nobody in the cove. He thought about fishing there first, but figured that the reservoir wouldn't be busy on a late Friday afternoon. He wouldn't go to the other end of the reservoir, but just three or four miles from the launching ramp and work his way back.

Within 15 minutes he arrived at his first spot. Bill had tried controlling boat drift with a trolling motor, but he had learned it was best for him to drop the anchor and anticipate where the boat would drift according to the wind direction and velocity. This allowed him to concentrate on how he was casting and presenting the bait to the fish. He had set up a Texas rig on the soft plastic stick bait called a senko and attached a small weight farther up the line. That would make the lure wiggle in the water like a large worm. He used a light weight because he didn't want the lure to sink quickly to the bottom. It was spring and bass were likely feeding at more shallow depths than they would in the warmer months of summer.

He took the rod, whipped it back a bit and cast it in a smooth arc over the water. That feeling of the first release of the line from the reel, arching over the water and plopping down 20 yards away was ecstatic and calming at the same time. He exhaled for what seemed to be the first time in weeks. Whatever happened in the days, months and years to come, he'd always have this beloved retreat.

37

Brad had been perching comfortably in his spot for about 20 minutes when the bow of Christenson's boat appeared at the cove's opening. As the boat skimmed across the opening, he saw Christenson turn his head and peer into the cove, no doubt assessing the conditions and searching for other anglers before moving on. His glance was brief and no cause for worry. Brad was confident that he was well hidden.

As the boat's wake began to disappear, Brad felt a brief pang of doubt. He knew that his plan had a lot more moving parts than Mikhail would have wanted. If it was up to Mikhail, Brad would have walked up to Christenson while he was still in his truck, asked an innocent question, then popped a bullet from the Python into his head. Since they didn't want the body discovered, he'd put it in the back of the Rav, throw a blanket over it, clean up the splatter in the truck cab and drive away, taking the body to a burial place in a wooded area of Anne Arundel County where Mikhail had a safe house.

Brad was a master of the safe and swift kill. He'd never been close to being caught. But, even though he had little ego—almost a prerequisite for his job—he had gotten bored with the routine hit. He'd gained a reputation for being reliable, but it was almost like being the kind of baseball pitcher who routinely had good outings and piled up the innings but never threw a shutout, much less a no hitter. Brad had made a very good living at his job, but he wanted something more. He was nearly 50 and thinking he might retire soon. He wanted what people in the trade called a *signature hit*.

He remembered the stories he heard from Jim Johnson, his mentor who taught him not only the skills but the mindset he needed to apply those skills for the best outcome. Jim saw it as a craft, with no room for showmanship, but once he saw Brad start to master myriad aspects of the job and after carefully parceling out stories of hits that went wrong because of poor planning or lack of caution, he allowed himself to tell Brad some stories of signature hits. These weren't widely known because there were no conventions of hit men; no trade shows with expositions of the latest tools or seminars like "Five Ways to Garrote in Full Public View" or "Poisoning Without Leaving a Trace." Still, word managed to spread underground through hitters and their apprentices. Brad imagined it was like how blues licks spread in the Delta during Robert Johnson's time.

Brad thought today could be his signature hit. Like when Charlie Obramowitz followed a guy for a few weeks knowing that every Sunday at 1 p.m. he would go to the Apex Theater in upper Fells Point and sit in the back row, where he could exit quickly after shooting his wad into a handkerchief, knowing no one would notice because the etiquette was to not pay attention to fellow patrons. In the middle of the feature, just as the guy was dribbling into the hanky, Charlie came up from behind, cupped one hand over the victim's mouth, slipped the wire around his neck with his other hand and pulled it tight until the man's head fell to his chest. Charlie pulled his hat over his eyes and quietly walked out, the woman in the ticket booth averting her eyes from him.

But now it had been nearly two hours since Christenson's boat had passed the cove on the way to other spots. Brad began to wonder if he'd overplayed his hand, something Jim Johnson had warned him against. Brad was thinking that if Christenson caught enough at his other spots he might not bother to fish the cove on his way back. Brad could still hit him with the powerful Ruger rifle as he passed by the cove, but the boat would be much farther away, it would be moving, Christenson would most likely be sitting, and he would be presenting a side profile instead of having his body facing Brad in a standing position. Nowhere near impossible, but a much greater challenge.

Brad tried to push these thoughts from his mind, harkening back to what Johnson had taught him: "Negative thoughts tend to be self-fulfilling prophecies." He'd learned to meditate over the last few years, so he closed his eyes, concentrating on even breathing and the inner workings of his body. He repeated a mantra he'd chosen from remembering a ninth-grade English teacher who told his class that the most beautiful word in the English language was *murmur*. Five minutes later, Brad opened his eyes to see the bow of Christenson's boat bend toward the opening of the cove. Brad exhaled in relief and set the Ruger on top of the stump.

38

Bill Christenson maneuvered the boat into the cove and threw the anchor overboard, where it pulled out about 15 or 20 feet of line before resting on the bottom. Judging by the wind direction he would probably drift to the spot where he wanted to fish within a minute or two. He pulled his rod from its holder, double-checked the rigging, and cast the line into the water about 20 yards from the shore. He had caught and released a few medium-sized smallmouths at his second spot, but was hoping for a couple of big ones before he called it a day.

As Christenson reeled in after his first cast, Brad Davenport trained the Ruger's fiber-optic sight on his heart, moving up to his neck and into his face and eyes. He didn't know why he did that. He'd been taught never to look at the eyes of a target. Instantly, Brad knew why: He saw unmistakable happiness.

Brad quickly moved the sight back down to Christenson's heart, but it was too late: His body bolted with a twinge like he'd never felt before. He might have felt a little flutter or a slight tick in the past, but never something like this. He pulled his eye away from the sight, took a deep breath, moved his torso slightly for better alignment, and returned his eye to the rim of the sight. Breathing out, he ever so gently squeezed the trigger. The gun emitted a fizzing sound like a soda can being opened after it was shaken. The bullet smacked into Christenson's chest, sending him falling back to the base of the elevated boat seat, his body folding against the seat and falling to the side of it.

Brad worked fast, sprinting down the hill, uncovering the kayak from the underbrush, and paddling out to the bass boat. He used the elastic cord on the bow of the kayak to secure it to the bass boat, spread out the tarp and placed it under Christenson. Fortunately, not much blood had yet seeped through Christenson's clothes and life jacket. He was a wiry guy with not much excess fat, which would help the body sink to the bottom and stay there. The cold water temperature would also help keep the body on the bottom.

After laying the body out on the tarp, Brad removed the keys, wallet and cell phone from Christenson's pockets, detached the fishing license clipped to the bottom of his jacket, pulled off the life jacket, and began lacerating Christenson in the neck, arm and legs, careful not to hit an artery that would send blood spattering. He thoroughly perforated the chest and abdominal cavities, going deep into the lungs and the intestines. When he thought he'd cut through the major places that would retain air in the body, he scooped up a couple handfuls of water and poured them into Christenson's mouth. He rolled the carcass tightly in the tarp and wrapped it securely with bungee cords. To provide additional weight, he pulled up the anchor, released the cleat that secured it to the boat, and wound it around the tarped body from head to toe. When he nearly ran out of rope, he secured the anchor to the body bag with two half hitches, dragged the bag to the side of the boat, and tipped it into the clear, cold water, watching it sink quietly to the bottom.

It was nothing but clean-up now, but Brad didn't let his concentration slip. He dipped the large sponge into the water and mopped up blood, some gristle and entrails from the deck of the bass boat. He kept soaking and wringing out the sponge so no blood would dry on it. When the deck was clean, he removed the rifle from the kayak and shot several times through the cockpit. He released the kayak from the bass boat and watched it fall through the water and disappear into the tall grass at the bottom.

As he pulled out of the cove into the open water, the only people he saw were a couple fishing from the shore about 50 yards from the launch site. Motoring past them in the middle of the reservoir, he gave a neighborly wave: Just another guy enjoying a day on the water. They gave him an odd-looking wave back, their hands looking as if they were making shadow puppets in the late afternoon air.

Brad returned to the launching pad, got the boat out of the water and onto the trailer, with no one to see him but the couple far away on the left shoreline. After securing the boat to the trailer, Brad climbed into Christenson's truck and started the powerful V8, which purred comfortingly, causing a nice ripple on the floorboards. He pulled out his cell and called Mikhail, who answered on the first ring.

"Tell me you have good news."

"Yes. It's done."

"Any snafus?"

"None. Airtight."

"And the remains?"

"Taken care of. I'm bringing his truck and the boat to the place in AA County. You'll need to pick up the Rav in the launching ramp parking lot at Pretty Boy."

"No worries. Thank you, Brad. It's nice to have someone to rely on. Speaking of which, could you hang around a few more days at your normal daily rate? We might have something else for you."

"Sure, I can do that. Might have a crab cake or two and maybe catch an O's game while I'm here."

"Whatever suits you. Just be ready."

"Always."

39

Joe Monroe was taking a nap after the long night and early morning when Bernard called. Normally he would be upset that his afternoon nap, a sacred ritual for a man his age, had been interrupted. But he was involved in a case, and when that happens sleep is secondary. He had no illusions about being a player in this thing with Bernard, but he was eager to help and hoping to get some inside intel that he might be able to use for a crime story of his own.

The assignment Bernard outlined was simple. Joe was to pick up Jackie Reynolds at the hospital and take him to a private rehab facility in the Mt. Vernon neighborhood. On the way there, Bernard asked Joe to try to get some more information about the abduction: Whether Buck had any outside connections, who they'd expected to pay the ransom, and anything else Joe could pry out of him.

The drug treatment facility had an odd name from Joe's perspective. It was called No Fear. Not Spring Hill or Fresh Air or Rebirth or Open Arms or Sunrise. Joe asked about the name and Bernard told him it was based on Eminem's song "Not Afraid," which talks about breaking out of his cage and facing his demons. Bernard said his friend Summers had told him about it. Summers had secretly entered the facility after his sophomore year in college, when his partying had led to a dalliance with cocaine. It was serious enough that Summers wasn't keeping up his conditioning and was saying he wouldn't be back at school to play in his junior year. When Joe asked if Summers is okay now, Bernard replied that he was in a good place, but it would always be day to day.

Joe pulled up to the hospital just as Jackie was walking out, looking around as if searching for a bus stop or an Uber. When Joe approached him, Jackie wasn't the compliant guy they'd taken to the hospital only hours ago.

"What are you doing here old timer?"

"The name's Joe Monroe, Mr. Reynolds, and I expect you to address me by my name. You seem not to be able to stand what they call prosperity. You're lucky that Bernard Jamal has some sympathy for your ass or you'd be spending time with some people who might not like the looks of you so much."

"I can take care of myself."

"You might think that, but look where you just came out of. Another 30 minutes in that car, you'd be dead as Prince. So get in this car and don't try to pull any games. I'm taking you to your home for the next three months, where Bernard says you'll have a nice room, some grounds to roam around, and three squares a day."

"Yeah, and who's going to pay for that?"

"Well, fortunately for you, you Andre-the-Giant-lookin'-muthafucka, Bernard has friends in high places, and you're going to be what they call the beneficiary of his largesse. Largesse being especially appropriate for your oversized ass."

"You always talk like this?"

"Only when dealing with a chucklehead."

"What if I say 'no' and just beat it out of here?"

"Look at you. Limping around on one leg with that bandage around your wrist and hand. Even if you had some mobility, where you going to go? We went to that shack on Benhill where you and your boy were holed up. That ain't no place to reside and you can't go back there anyway. That neighbor you stole electricity from ain't so happy."

"Was Buck there?"

"No, smelled like he was there recently, but he was gone by the time we got there. Now get in the car."

"Okay, I'll come along, but rehab doesn't stick with me. If I don't like it, I'm out of there."

"Suit yourself, but I wouldn't want to read about you in the *Sunpapers* next week. So settle down and relax. I have some casual questions to ask on our way to your new home."

"Shit, just what I need. A Black Sherlock Holmes."

"More like Easy Rawlins, son."

40

At 4 p.m. that afternoon Bernard, Tony and Charlaine sat down on the picnic tables in the back lot of DII headquarters. It was a warm, breezy day, the last one before a cold front was expected over the weekend. Bernard had sent Charlaine an outline of everything that had happened: Details on the abduction, his talks with Prisha and Roland, what he and Joe had found out about Jackie and Buck, and who Bernard considered competitors, although he stressed that he couldn't imagine anyone harboring any ill will toward anyone at TripleDouble or 3Make. Bernard said the 3D printing industry was fairly circumscribed, and despite being competitive, all the players wanted essentially the same thing: To bring 3D printing into the mainstream for engineering, manufacturing and healthcare industries. According to Bernard, there was enough pie for everyone to have a healthy slice.

Joe Monroe had briefed Bernard on his conversation with Jackie Reynolds, who reiterated that he knew of no other people involved in the failed abduction scheme. Tony remained skeptical.

"I don't think this Reynolds guy is lying per se, but it's perfectly logical that Buck, the alleged brains of this operation, wouldn't share his pertinents with a guy he hired to do his thug work. Same with the redhead girl. But, I'm willing to find this Buck and shake him like a lemon tree; see what falls. You know what I say about coincidences."

"Yes, I know, Tony, but we don't need to clog Bernard's pretty head with your wisdom at this point," said Charlaine. "What do we want to do from the 3Make angle? Sounds like this Ohtari might be a person of interest, especially since he's had shady dealings in the past; the kind that could have gotten him arrested if his previous employer was so inclined."

"I definitely want you to look into him, but first I'd like to see what's going on in that nightshift lab," said Bernard. "I hate to sound self-serving, but if something illegal is going on, 3Make, and by extension TripleDouble, could be in deep shit. Roland talked to Christenson, who said he thinks it's just a misunderstanding with Prisha. Christenson took off early today and said he'd talk to a couple of his guys involved in the nightshift research on Monday morning. But even if he thinks nothing is going on, how do you explain someone having you tail Prisha?"

"I'm hoping our IT expert can help get to the bottom of that," said Tony. "But meantime, can we get entry into that nightshift lab to poke around?"

"I can get the combination to the door lock," said Bernard, "but I'm not sure what we'd be looking for. Roland told me he's coming into town on Monday morning, but I think he might cause some commotion within the engineering crew if he starts snooping around."

"How about the cleaning crew?" asked Charlaine. "I'm sure they come in at night after hours."

"Yeah, but I wouldn't want them involved," said Bernard. "And again, they wouldn't know what to look for. I'm not even sure I'd know what to look for."

"You wouldn't have to know," said Charlaine. "We could video the scene and then you and Roland could see if there is anything that looks suspicious."

"Who's this 'we'?" asked Tony.

"It's known as the royal we, Tone," replied Charlaine. "And I've played the role of cleaning lady before in an off-Broadway audition in the very building we're sitting behind."

There was a second or two of silence, then the light came on in Tony's eyes.

"You're going to do a reprisal of the cleaning lady role, right Goddess? But this time on the nightshift stage!"

"Can't get much by you, Tone."

Two hours later, Charlaine came home to find Joy at the stove stirring risotto with one hand while the other held a full glass of white wine. A pile of freshly grilled shrimp sat nearby in a bowl on the countertop. Charlaine was still in work mode until Joy beamed that smile at her from across the kitchen.

"Can I get you a cold glass of something to kick off the weekend?"

"I wish, you darling you, but I have an assignment tonight. Need to head out again around seven."

"How long will you be? I had planned on watching that new Bosch season that starts tonight. What's it this time?"

"Gotta do some undercover at 3Make. I figure I'll be back by around 9 if everything goes as planned."

"If everything goes as planned," Joy repeated, the skepticism tightening her throat. "Are you expecting anything dangerous?"

"No, maybe some nerds noodling around with some 3D printing stuff, but I doubt I'll run into anybody. Strictly looking around and taking some videos. The place will probably be empty, being Friday night and whatnot." Charlaine trying to be casual about it.

Joy's face fell, a sight that sunk Charlaine's heart. In many ways, they were a perfect couple. They could talk for hours. They made love passionately and frequently. They had a mutual love of books, movies, food and Baltimore sports. But Joy treated the danger of Charlaine's job as an interloper into their otherwise serene lives. Charlaine treated it like part of life. A level of danger had always been in Charlaine's life. She might not welcome it, but she faced it head on and tried to conquer any fear associated with it.

Joy had no problem detaching from her work. When she had vacation time, she wanted adventure: cruises, camping, travels to Europe or South America. On the go with an itinerary that would bring even the most ardent adventurers to their knees. Charlaine wanted nothing more than to go to Ocean City and spend her time on the beach with a good book.

Charlaine tried not to extrapolate a future of regularly dashing Joy's expectations, but it was sometimes hard to see alternative scenarios given the people they were. And in Charlaine's experience, people can adjust but they rarely change from their core beings.

Charlaine thought that maybe they should get the dog that Joy wanted: At least she'd have some companionship for times like these.

41

Mikhail sighed in relief after hanging up with Davenport. A loose end taken care of. Just two more things to handle, and they'd be in good shape.

First thing was to have Barrett and Chen pull out of 3Make. They had all they needed: The design of the gun, the recipe and process for creating the new materials needed for mass production of the gun shell and ammo, and the procedures for producing large quantities of the single-part revolver shells within a single run. Now, they just had to share their work with their partners around the globe, first collecting what Mikhail was calling a "finder's fee." He thought they should get Barrett and Chen out of 3Make as soon as possible, taking assets and incriminating evidence with them, such as the prototype guns and materials stowed away in a locked storage cabinet within the nightshift lab. He didn't want Roland coming in on his own and snooping around.

The other loose end was Ohtari. He had to disappear, one way or another. Mikhail didn't like the odds of him inadvertently giving something away and causing suspicion. Ohtari thought he could talk his way out of anything. What did one of the Dutch partners say about him? Oh, yeah, *he thinks butter melts in his mouth, but if you pressure him, he'll spit it out.* Ohtari had already shown his lack of discretion by visiting the nightshift lab and being seen by Prisha Kapoor.

Mikhail was going to make a magnanimous offer to Ohtari, but not give him an alternative. Either Ohtari would take his offer to relocate with a new identity and a payoff that could keep him modestly comfortable for the rest of his life, or Mikhail would arrange a permanent exit for him. It was up to Ohtari to play the right card. Mikhail didn't care one way or another. Pay to relocate him or pay to have him dispatched. Two sides of the same coin.

There were others that could be problematic if they learned too much. Roland was the most worrisome because he was the most likely candidate for unraveling The Helix scheme. He knew too much for Mikhail's comfort, but as long as he didn't meddle any further he was relatively safe. Same for Bernard Jamal, the VC guy. Same for the investigation agency, DII. They might be bothered by not being able to fully connect the dots, but they didn't have unlimited resources to continue pursuing the case.

Mikhail was also busy planting false clues about Christenson's disappearance. After the hit at Pretty Boy, two of his guys used Christenson's keys to enter the house and pack one of his suitcases full of clothes from his closet. With his car, boat, clothes and suitcase gone, investigators could easily draw the conclusion that Mikhail had set them up to draw; that Christenson had fled from an increasingly unhappy life.

As for Barrett and Chen, they would each tender their resignations via email, the content of which would be a bit ambiguous, but common: Found a new opportunity too good to refuse. The two friends had never fully integrated into the 3Make culture, so it would be perfectly logical that they took off without advance notice. It could easily be assumed, Mikhail thought, that Barrett and Chen were in league with Ohtari, which could prompt investigators to pursue that lead at the expense of other avenues. Mikhail found that once investigators settled on a scenario, they would bend pieces of evidence to fit within it. People, especially Americans, want simple explanations, Mikhail thought, and they'll do almost anything to make the pieces of the puzzle fit.

The other red herring was something that Mikhail didn't arrange: Those two guys trying to kidnap Jamal. Man, was that a piece of unplanned luck; a diversion that Mikhail didn't have to plant. He could kiss those two guys.

42

Brad Davenport was uncharacteristically edgy. Everything had gone as planned with the job and he was driving back down 183 toward the Baltimore Beltway that circled the city. It was rush hour and traffic was moving in fits and starts. He didn't know why but he felt curiously visible; a unique feeling for a guy who could disappear into any situation. He wasn't handsome nor homely. His clothes told no story. He wasn't too short or too tall. Not fat or skinny. He would be described as average. Didn't have any accent; well, maybe a slight Southern one from growing up in Virginia, but not too different from anyone else in the Delmarva area.

At first he thought he was hungry. He hadn't eaten since he stopped to get a biscuit before picking up the SUV, guns and ammo at the place in Anne Arundel County where he was now headed. He thought about stopping somewhere for a bite, but didn't want anybody else to see him. There was no reason for thinking that someone might notice him. Just another guy returning home from fishing. But he couldn't risk it. Then he remembered he'd bought some jerky at Dick's and pulled it from his jacket pocket, took a big bite and gnawed at it.

But after he'd devoured a couple of sticks of jerky, he still felt nervous. He'd always thought he was nearly devoid of feelings, rarely afraid, angry, happy or sad. It bothered him when he was in his early teens, when he was known as David Pearson, his surname coming from his adoptive parents. He saw people cry at things that didn't move him at all. He remembered seeing the reports of the mass shooting at a McDonalds in San Ysidro, California. Twenty one were killed and 19 wounded. His adoptive parents wept while watching the news that night. He felt nothing except a bit of titillation over the power the killer must have felt.

His adoptive parents took care of the basics but their kids were never loved. They were adopted because of the government funding the Pearsons received. There were five kids in the household while David was there. The two oldest boys worked in the old man's gas station and convenience store and the girls did odd jobs around the house and worked at the Tasty Freeze, the local diner, the hardware store, fast food places or anywhere else they could get work once they turned 15. The Pearsons fed the local economy with the cheap labor of their adopted children over the years and the locals were grateful for it. The kids were considered laborers and money makers, and any education beyond high school was not offered or expected.

The boy known as David Pearson met his mentor when he was 18. David was out of high school and working 14-hour days at a bait shop when he met Jim Johnson. Johnson said he'd just moved to the area and was looking for a fishing guide. When he wasn't working, David would take a single-engine skiff around the Elizabeth River and its tributaries, fishing the local waters for black drum, spotted sea trout, croaker, flounder, gray trout, red puppy drum, striped bass, and tautog. Johnson asked David to show him the best spots. He said he would make it well worth David's time and he did, paying him twice what he made in a 14-hour day at the bait shop.

At first, the time on the water was awkward for David, who didn't know anything about conversation. The children in the Pearson household didn't say much other than "no ma'am" and "yes sir." What was there to say? The work they did was trivial and mostly didn't require talking. They were the kind of rote jobs where nothing much exceptional happened. At the dinner table, neither parent embraced anything beyond normal reporting of how the day went, usually limited to a few words. The rare times one of David's sisters ventured a story about something unusual that happened at work, their mother would cut them short with the admonition to give some peace and quiet to their father, who has to listen to people all day. David knew this wasn't true, as his father was nearly as intolerant of conversation at the gas station and convenience store as he was at home.

Out on the water, Jim Johnson kept plying David with questions, stuff that nobody ventured to ask: How did he learn all he knew about fishing? How'd he figure out that rigging on the bait line? What did he think of that young pitcher who just joined the Norfolk Tides, the one who was destined to be a future number one starter for the Orioles? What was he going to do now that he'd graduated from high school? David knew he wanted to get away from the Pearsons, and figured he might eventually join the Navy, but that was the extent of his plans.

When October rolled around, Johnson invited David to go duck hunting with him. With his keen eye and ability to discern patterns in nature, David was a natural. He had an innate calmness and a steady hand, making him an excellent shooter. Without consciously knowing it at first, Johnson was grooming his replacement.

Within a year, David had earned Johnson's trust and the veteran hit man started to open up, telling him about places he traveled for his job, although still not revealing what exactly he did for a living. But David was getting closer to Johnson, as close as he'd been to anyone, and the older man began telling him stories and revealing tricks of the trade. Johnson didn't swear David to secrecy because he knew the young man had no one with whom to confide: Johnson was the closest thing he'd had to a father and David would never do anything to compromise his mentor's trust, something that remained in place until Johnson's death two years ago.

Creeping along the Beltway toward the Glen Burnie exit, Brad had a feeling similar to the emotions that welled in him when Johnson died. He'd made a mistake that he knew better than to make. He should have never lifted that rifle sight to Bill Christenson's eyes. Because what he saw there, as best he knew about it, was not only happiness, but serenity, something he'd first seen on Jim Johnson's face in the fading light of day on the water near the Indian River Bridge. When Brad saw Johnson's face in his mind's eye, he identified what was gnawing at him: shame. Shame not borne of shooting Christenson, but of his need for the signature hit. He remembered something that Johnson had quoted to him from the bible: *Pride goeth before the fall.*

43

Spencer Ohtari pulled into the parking lot of his condo, just north of the city in Towson. He'd moved there after losing his job at Sintology. His wife of 21 years had left him and his two adult children made it known that they no longer wanted anything to do with him.

Ohtari thought that his wife leaving him was a godsend. He was in his late 40s and considered handsome and fit. He lifted at the Y three days a week and played tennis at least twice a week, outdoors in the warmer months and indoors at the racket club when it got too cold to play outdoors.

He did the dating apps after the divorce was finalized and at first it was exciting: A sea of women from which to choose; different sizes, shapes, cultures, backgrounds and interests. But none of them stuck for him. They were looking for someone with a job to which they could relate, and Spencer couldn't tell them what he was doing. From time to time, his resentment toward his wife and children came through—not a good look for a potential partner. He also found that he wasn't too tolerant of beliefs that ran contrary to his, so the middle earther was abandoned once she shared her beliefs, as was the God Squad woman who was the devil incarnate in the sack.

Even the idea of the condo had started to sour for Spencer. People are okay until you live cheek and jaw with them. Then you find that they tramp up and down the hall in the units above yours, play their music at ear-splitting volumes, cheer and stomp loudly every Sunday when the Ravens are on TV, and allow their pets to do their business everywhere and anywhere on the condo grounds without picking up after them.

Spencer was walking up the steps to the second floor landing juggling a couple of grocery bags, one with two bottles of Chardonnay and the other containing a box of chicken and sides from Royal Farms. He had the wine bag braced against his hip as he dug in his pocket for his keys when his door opened from inside and out stepped Mikhail to take the Royal Farms bag from his right hand. Spencer nearly dropped the wine bag.

"Surprise," said Mikhail with a wide grin. "What did you get us for dinner?"

Spencer struggled to regain his composure and brushed by Mikhail into the kitchen, plopping the bag of wine onto the counter next to the refrigerator. He took a deep breath and calmed himself.

"How did you get in here? And what are you doing here?"

Mikhail chuckled like a man thinking of a long-standing joke.

"One thing at a time, my friend. Anyone with a bit of skill can get into a place like this, and I'm nothing if not skilled."

Spencer didn't like this new-found haughtiness in Mikhail. He couldn't pinpoint when it started, but lately the guy who used to be humble was acting superior. Treating Spencer like a subordinate. Did he forget who put this scheme together? Who made all the connections that made it possible?

"You could have called first; given me a heads up. I could have grilled us some steaks; treated you to a proper meal."

"You don't have to go out of your way for me, my friend. Besides, all I've seen since I've come to Baltimore are ads for this world-famous Royal Farms chicken. I think it would go down a treat with that nice Chardonnay."

"I'm surprised, that's all. I thought we're not supposed to be seen together, unless it's in private with our, ummm, associates."

"Well, since you mention it Spence, you've touched on a little issue about which we associates are concerned."

Spencer pulled his back up and jutted his chest out.

"What issue? I haven't heard anything."

Mikhail found a corkscrew in a cabinet drawer and deftly opened one of the wine bottles with a gentle pop. He gave Spencer a pitying look.

"You've not heard anything about it because you are part of the issue, Spencer. Specifically, your visibility in these environs. But no worries, because I have a choice offering for you, one almost as appealing as that box of Royal Farms chicken."

"You're offering *me* a choice? Since when were you in charge of this operation?"

"Since you botched the last job. You just didn't know it until now."

Spencer's face went blank, his features frozen for a second and his eyes practically bulging out of their sockets. He took a moment to gather himself, then spoke in measured tones.

"Excuse me if I don't take your word for it, Mikhail, or whatever the fuck your name really is. I'll just check with my people in China and Russia to straighten out what is surely a misunderstanding."

Mikhail smiled, or more accurately, lifted the edge of his lips in an upright direction. The rest of his face stayed stone-like.

"Check with them all you want, you'll get no confirmation one way or the other. The fact is, I'm here, now, in front of you with a proposition."

Spencer shook his head as if to clear cobwebs.

"I don't understand why you're doing this. You'll have enough money to lay around on a beach the rest of your life if you wanted to. Hell, you could buy your own fuckin' island."

Mikhail made a tut-tut sound, as if he was showing disappointment in a toddler.

"Your visibility makes you a liability, no rhyme intended. And since you're superfluous to the operation, everyone decided that it's time for your removal."

"Everyone? That's not possible! What about Barrett and Chen? I brought them into this thing."

"Barrett and Chen don't know about this and they're unlikely to care. Do you remember how you got them into this? Through sheer greed and self-interest. They care as much about you as they do about screwing 3Make. I'll tell them their share has increased and they'll be absolutely delighted."

"Is this some kind of test?" Spencer was practically snarling now.

"No test. You already failed the test, Spencer. I'm giving you two choices. And you have exactly 24 hours to make a decision. Either choice is a form of permanent retirement, one fairly pleasant, the other not so much. You're fortunate to get a choice. Christenson didn't get one."

Spencer plopped down on the sofa and put his hands over his reddened face.

"What happened to Christenson? He knew nothing. What the fuck did I do to deserve this? What did I do to you or anyone else?"

Mikhail pursed his lips and shook his head slowly back and forth.

"Too many questions and too late for explanations, Spence. Now here are the choices..."

44

Bernard pulled into the diagonal parking space in front of his house and took a deep breath. He had been listening to some old-school soul, the kind his grandmother played around the house when he was growing up. "Tell Me This Is a Dream" by the Delfonics came on and he heard it out. It seemed appropriate for his situation. Not with Kensey, but with things not being what they seemed. He too wished it was a dream.

As he listened to the song, the words of which he knew by heart from singing them with his grandmother, he thought he needed to try to get back to some form of normality when he entered the house. Kensey deserved it after what she'd been through. Bernard often thought that when misfortune, physical or mental, visited a person that it was that person's loved ones who suffered the most. It reminded him of another song, one from Isaac Hayes and David Porter, made into a hit by Sam and Dave: "When something is wrong with my baby, something is wrong with me…" Bernard needed to convince Kensey that he wasn't in any danger; that what happened last night was a fluke.

But as much as he tried to put last night's events behind him, different aspects of the situation kept bubbling to the surface. He didn't like the idea of Charlaine going into the nightshift lab in disguise. He didn't think there was any danger, but who knew? He thought the attempted abduction was just the crackpot idea of two guys desperate for money, as Jackie said it was. But what if it was something more? He didn't have the luxury to be casual about it, just as Stacy Greer didn't have the luxury to turn his back on that guy in the playground after shit-talking him the entire afternoon. But he also refused to live in fear or to force his partner to live that way.

He walked up three brick steps that used to be marble, took another deep breath, put the key in the lock, and opened the front door. He was hit with the aroma of frying fish and remembered it was Friday night, a night he and Kensey normally set aside for low-key celebration. A movie or a ball game on TV. A bit more wine than usual. Love making. No matter how high they got up the corporate ladder, they treated Friday like blue-collar workers, saluting the end of the work week and relishing the next two days off.

Bernard walked through the narrow hallway to the back of the house, where the kitchen looked out into the small, fenced in backyard about 20 feet wide and 30 feet deep. The postage-stamp backyard didn't bother them, as both were used to using public space for recreation. Patterson Park was just three blocks away and that was enough of a getaway. There was also a full-length pool and fully stocked workout facility at the fitness club downtown.

Bernard put his briefcase on the floor next to the kitchen table, and went over to the stove, where Kensey turned to greet him. She looked tired but managed a smile. When he held her, everything felt right. Her curves fit in his crevices, eliminating any awkwardness caused by their difference in height.

"So, is this a victory celebration for your new client?"

"Not quite—it turned out to be a little more than that."

Bernard pulled back a bit, cradling her lower spine in his interlocked hands.

"How so?" Bernard went soft inside when she looked up at him with those big blues.

"They want me to join the company. To leave the agency for a full-time gig with them, working under Summers."

Bernard raised his eyebrows and grinned.

"I hope they phrased it differently than 'working under Summers'."

Kensey laughed and smacked him on the ass with a dish towel.

"Leave it to you, Bernard Jamal, to think of a sexual connotation."

"I'm thinking of a variety of sexual connotations at the moment."

"Yeah, I think I'm feeling what you're feeling." Kensey bumped her groin against his swelling and held it there for a few seconds. "But you know fried fish tastes best right out of the pan. I've also fried up some of those giant onion rings you love so much. So, maybe we delay one gratification for another? One appetite for another?"

She gently pushed him away and turned back to the stove. He sighed and put his arms around her waist from behind.

"When did you become such a mature adult? The kind who can talk of delayed gratification?"

"Someone needs to be the adult in this household. Plus, we have all night, right?"

"Yes, all night. I don't plan on getting abducted two nights in a row."

"Good thing; a woman can only take so much of that shit."

45

Colin Barrett was not one for introspection.

He was 27 years old, only a few years away from getting his masters at Johns Hopkins' Whiting School of Engineering. He'd started working at Sintology when he was still in school, one of the best and brightest Hopkins had to offer. He had no real relationships aside from his friendship with Jimmy Chen, whom he met upon joining 3Make.

Colin had always been a loner, without any outside interests except for some forays into online gaming. But he didn't feel part of any gaming community, and he had no special reverence for the creators or players of online games. He just did it to kill time. It was a passion for Chen. Colin recognized that and didn't poke fun at his older friend's almost comic devotion to Fortnight and Dota.

Sometimes Colin wished he was passionate about something outside of work, but nothing ever caught on with him. He was the equivalent of a cultural rambler, investigating different things—music, film, art, TV, sci fi books—and then moving on when none of them fully engaged him.

What he loved was taking complex assemblies and reinventing them as one piece that could be turned into reality with 3D printing. That's how he got Spencer Ohtari's attention at Sintology. What others thought of as dizzyingly complex seemed simple to Colin. He didn't know it was a special skill at first, perhaps because it was with him always—he solved a Rubik's Cube at age five and put together entire Lego cities at age seven.

His father was a satellite engineer at Northrop Grumman and his mother a bioscience researcher at University of Maryland College Park. Neither had much of a taste for active parenting, sending Colin and his sister to a series of private schools whose administrators and teachers acted as surrogate parents. His sister met lifelong friends in high school and college, but Colin could never make himself fit in with any one group, not even the nerds in the robotics club. Not that he made much of an effort.

Part of Colin's social problem, if you wanted to call it that, was he had little inclination to share thoughts, listen to others' opinions, or pursue any outside activities that required teamwork. His parents thought that this was perfectly normal; in fact, practically ideal for their purposes. It was high praise for his mother to characterize Colin as "a perfect grown up when he was a kid."

When he started at Sintology, Colin was pleased to find that most of the engineers in the company felt like he did: They socialized at the minimum level required for the job. At company parties, the engineers were typically found off in a corner, waiting for the earliest moment in which they could leave.

Colin wasn't dour or foreboding, just detached and uninterested. Some women found him attractive—he was a small, compact man with fine features, a shock of auburn hair, and long eyelashes that exuded a Bambi-like cuteness—but he had no interest in the commitment a relationship requires. As for sex, he found it baffling that people could be so consumed with the exchange of fluids.

What motivated Colin was recognition for his work in the form of money. What he would do with the money, nobody knew. He didn't crave big houses, expensive cars or clothes, or a trophy wife. He didn't seem to want anything material but money itself, enough so he could do exactly what he wanted. Chen wanted money too, but he wanted it for the same reason as most men: To buy things that other people would envy.

Spencer recognized that burning desire in the short time Colin was at Sintology. He never enlisted Colin in his scheme to source illegal materials, but the young engineer was always on his radar. He'd seen that Colin could visualize designs for 3D printing that others couldn't even conceptualize, much less develop into a fully functional part or product. Colin even rewrote large swaths of the company's computer-aided design software to accommodate the unique capabilities of 3D printing technology. Looking to the future, Spencer encouraged Colin, putting him in charge of the software R&D team at Sintology. Despite his young age and lack of management skills, Colin was paid beyond what engineers with 10 more years of experience were making.

When he was let go by Sintology, Spencer urged Colin to leave that company and join 3Make. He told Colin that he would never get what he wanted at Sintology; that older engineers would always seek to keep him down. At 3Make, Colin could make a top-of-the-line salary and also pursue independent projects arranged by Ohtari, doubling the money he could make at Sintology.

Colin had already sensed resentment among the older Sintology engineers, so it was no leap in logic to believe Spencer. Besides, Colin was nearing 30, and felt internal pressure to get further down the path to complete autonomy. What sealed the deal is that during his interview with 3Make, Colin met Chen. While flashing neon lights didn't go off, both parties knew they had something the other wanted. Chen was the materials expert that Colin needed to turn his designs into reality, and Colin could provide the designs that maximized the potential for Chen's material innovations.

It was easier than Spencer thought to persuade Colin to pursue The Helix project. Colin had little or no moral compass. He just wanted his creations to get out into the world. Who paid for the work was of no concern to him. Nor was it difficult for Colin, despite his limited facility with words, to bring Chen on board. Chen was 33 and wanted to get away from the grind while still young, with enough cash to retire to Thailand or Vietnam. He dreamed of owning a bachelor's pad and a fast car, keeping a stable of women, plying himself with the best weed, and competing in the upper echelons of the gaming world for the rest of his life.

Colin didn't think much about it when Mikhail called and told him that Spencer was out of the picture. That was three hours ago. Thirty minutes ago, Spencer called him, but Colin didn't answer. He thought that Spencer would give him a bunch of crap about loyalty, which to Colin's mind never bought anyone anything that he could see. Chen didn't value it much either; it was in his nature to view everyone but Colin as a competitive rival.

After he and Chen emailed their resignations to Christenson, and cleared out the designs, prototypes and materials from the nightshift lab tonight, Colin would get a new phone with a new number. He knew Chen would do the same without giving another thought to Spencer Ohtari. Neither would have any compunction about leaving 3Make either. Both knew that there would be some collateral damage along the way to their self-defined destinies, and they were fine with that. As Spencer himself once said to Colin, "you might have to step over some bodies on your way to the top." Colin almost laughed at the fact that one of those bodies would be Spencer's.

46

Charlaine left around 7 for the half-hour drive to 3Make headquarters in Locust Point. Bernard Jamal had given her pass codes to the building and the warning not to engage with anyone she might run into at the nightshift lab, although he didn't expect anyone to be there on a Friday night.

She wore baggy sweats, Skechers, a flowered smock, rubber gloves, and one new piece of gear, a turban-like head wrap accented on the front with what looked like a button but was actually a bluetooth camera. Charlaine hadn't yet used the camera on an assignment, but she had tested it several times, walking around town wearing the turban to see whether it would attract undue attention. People looked at her, because they always did, but their gaze was typically drawn elsewhere; in the case of men, usually to her backside.

The mode of dress wasn't the only disguise. She had a capped front tooth with a gold star etched into it and she took on the sweet demeanor of a woman named Tina who worked the counter of the liquor store in the West Baltimore neighborhood where Charlaine grew up. Tina never had much in the way of clothes, nor was she especially attractive, but she had a dazzling grin and a special greeting for every customer, calling the women "Sweetie" and the men "Sugar." She radiated joy, even behind the foggy plexiglass window that spanned the checkout counter. People felt better when they encountered Tina, even if they were purchasing a pint with shaky hands holding their last bit of cash.

Charlaine pulled her car into the 3Make lot and was relieved to find it empty. No stragglers at the start of a nice spring weekend close to summer. People were no doubt grilling at home, watching the O's game airing from Detroit, or prepping for a night on the town. Normal stuff. Charlaine didn't envy them. She wouldn't substitute the adrenaline that was coursing through her for anything. *You a stone-cold junkie*, she said to herself in her Tina-like voice, as she pulled on the rubber gloves and retrieved her trash can on wheels, a large push broom, and a dustpan from the back of the Forester.

There was an entrance to the nightshift lab at the back of the building, an unmarked door that adjoined a loading dock. Charlaine entered the pass code and stepped inside a room about half the size of a basketball court. There were a few metal benches strewn with various parts, cleaning implements, and boxes of granular materials. Two large machines and what looked like cleaning stations lined the walls. Everything was out in the open except for a large storage cabinet the size of a double refrigerator that sat on the same wall as the door through which Charlaine entered. Charlaine turned on the video camera and its microphone and walked slowly around the area.

She hardly recognized anything she saw. There was something that looked like a shower head except for many more spray holes arrayed in concentric circles. There was a sort of manifold, but with pipes snaking across one another in intricate patterns; when she picked up the part, it was surprisingly lightweight, like those sneakers with foam soles. There were brackets shaped like butterflies and what looked like elaborate transparent molds. A black plastic part looked like a heating/air conditioning vent for a car.

Although she hated the word that everyone used for anything unusual, *surreal* came to mind. It looked like the laboratory of a scientist with a slightly warped mind, like that Escher poster Joy had in her studio. Charlaine videoed everything, sometimes picking up parts and commenting on their weight and texture.

When she had traversed the entire lab she stopped in front of the cabinet, which had a sticker on the door with "Barrett/Chen" written on it. The handle to the cabinet was secured by a common combination lock. She was thinking about cracking the lock using a methodology she'd learned online and practiced on her own. It was a fairly simple procedure of putting some pressure on the loop part and dialing until finding a bit of looseness on a particular number. She could normally open this type of lock in five to 10 minutes. But the moment she placed her hand on the lock she heard footsteps outside the door and muted conversation. She backed away from the cabinet and retrieved her broom and trash can on wheels just as two small men entered the lab.

She looked up from the broom about the same time the two men spotted her about 10 feet away.

"Oh, you two scared me!" she said in a high-pitched voice, holding her hand over her heart and fluttering her eyelashes. "Almost gave me a heart attack. I was supposed to be alone in here."

The slightly bigger of the two, a kinda cute white dude with long, curly hair, gave Charlaine a hard look. Bernard had given her pictures of the engineering staff so she knew that he was Barrett. The other one was Chen.

"What are you doing here? Don't you know this is a restricted area?"

"Don't worry, Sugar," Charlaine cooed. "I won't bother y'all none. I don't even know what this stuff is. I'm just here to sweep and mop the floors, Honey, then I'll be on my way. What are you two handsome gentlemen doin' here on a Friday night, anyway?"

"That's none of your business," Barrett snarled, but then the Asian-looking guy, Chen, stepped up and smiled. Charlaine recognized the look. A self-defined ladies' man. She had something to work with here. The guy wasn't too bad looking. Trim, with a nice pair of AG jeans, a fitted

Hawaiian shirt, black-and-white Jordans, and neatly cut, thick black hair. His skin was slightly lighter than Charlaine's. He turned to his partner and patted him on the shoulder.

"C'mon Colin, no need to be harsh with the lady. She's just doing her job."

Barrett wasn't giving in.

"I don't want her here, Jimmy. Nobody's supposed to be here after hours."

Charlaine leaned on her broom and gave her best sympathetic look.

"Looky here, Sugar, I'm sorry I upset you. I'll be out of your gorgeous hair in a minute. Just let me finish my sweepin' and I'll come back to mop up later when y'all have left."

Barrett was having none of it.

"Naw. Doesn't work that way. You. Leave. Now."

Charlaine took a step back and put her hands up as if she was surrendering, the second time in two nights she had to make that move. She swallowed her anger, calmed the churning in her stomach, and once again summoned the sweet Tina persona.

"Okay Sugar, okay, I'm out of here, but I hope I don't get in trouble with my boss man. I'll just let myself out that back door there."

Barrett shook his head.

"No you don't. You go out the front door and exit at the front of the building. Then get in your car and leave. I don't want to see you on the premises while we're here."

"Okay, okay, Sugar, whatever you want. You two have a blessed evening, you hear?"

47

Charlaine paused outside the inner door to the nightshift lab and thought about her next move. She'd had the turban camera on during her exchange with Barrett and Chen. She couldn't verify for certain that the two were up to something shady, but the way Barrett reacted made her suspicious.

She wished she had brought another camera to leave inside the lab. There were security cameras mounted on all four upper corners of the lab, but Charlaine had noticed that they were turned off. She wondered if security was aware of that fact, or if the engineers working in the nightshift lab had disabled the cameras themselves. Barrett and Chen didn't look dangerous, but Charlaine didn't want to confront them if they were just innocent engineers who didn't have anything better to do on a Friday night. She could see Barrett working on a Friday night, but not Chen: Charlaine was certain he was the kind to be chasing tail on a Friday night in the city. Barrett appeared to be the guy in charge, but that kind of dynamic was often deceiving. Sometimes the seemingly nice guy was the one holding the cards.

There were no windows looking into the lab so Charlaine couldn't peek in to see what Barrett and Chen were doing. She left her cleaning equipment in the foyer and ran out the front door and around the side of the building to the back parking lot.

Charlaine's Forester was the only car in the lot, but a panel truck was parked with its back against the loading dock. Barrett and Chen would probably be looking for Charlaine's car in the back lot, so she drove around to the front and out of the parking lot to the nearest space where she could park. It was an industrial area with no other cars around, but her car looked like one that could have broken down and been abandoned temporarily.

Charlaine flipped up the hatchback of the Forester and opened a locked box, pulling out a few things she hoped not to need, including a folding knife and her Glock 22. She ran around the side of the building, cursing herself for her heavy breathing. She'd been working too many hours and not paying attention to her conditioning. Joy was a walker and biker, and Charlaine had frequently accompanied her on rides and walks around Lake Monticello. But lately she'd come home too tired to do anything but some weightlifting and a brief stint on the elliptical in the basement.

There was a line of shrubs parallel to the back of the building, ending where the loading dock jutted out at a 90-degree angle. The rolling door of the panel truck backed up against the dock was open about a foot.

There was just enough room to squeeze between the back wall of the building and the outer leaves of the shrubs, as long as Charlaine didn't mind getting stabbed by the pointy edges of the ivy-like leaves. She did mind, plenty, but the gig often led to these kinds of situations. At least it wasn't wasps or snakes, or the inside of a dumpster, the charms of which Charlaine had experienced at one point or another in her PI career.

Charlaine walked slowly sideways through the narrow clearing, placing her arms above her head and pressing her back against the wall. The scratches of the brick and mortar against her back and upper arms were preferable to the needle pricks of the shrubs' thick leaves. When she got to the intersection of the wall and the loading dock, she ducked down under the four-foot-high landing.

As she peeked over the edge of the landing, the lab door flew open and a flat-bed cart containing several boxes rolled out into the concrete surface.

Charlaine ducked under the landing just as Chen appeared behind the cart. He rolled the cart to the edge of the dock, quickly unloaded the boxes into the back of the truck, and wheeled the empty cart back inside.

Charlaine decided to take a chance. She pulled a magnetic GPS device with built-in batteries out of the pocket of her smock, jumped up and pulled herself onto the dock. She scooted to the side of the truck, jumped down from the dock and landed in a crouch beside the passenger-side back wheel. She affixed the GPS device to the inside of the wheel well, and ran back to her position on the side of the loading dock. Colin and Jimmy came out a minute later, loading the truck with a second round of boxes.

Moments after they closed the door, a recent model Mercedes pulled into the lot and parked next to the panel truck. Charlaine ducked behind the shrubs as a tall, slender man got out of the car, not bothering to turn off the ignition or headlights. He rushed around the side of the panel truck, leapt up the steps on the other side of the dock, entered the pass code and slung the back door open, the door slamming shut behind him.

Charlaine heard conversation inside, but the lab door was heavy and she couldn't make out what the men were saying. She kept pressed against the wall, her heart dancing. Five minutes later, Barrett and Chen appeared and quickly emptied another load of boxes into the truck. When they were done they rolled the cart back into the lab, keeping the door propped open with one of the boxes. Charlaine could hear them working inside, hurrying and speaking in frantic whispers. Within minutes they appeared with another cartload of boxes, quickly unloading them into the truck, and returning the cart to the lab. Several seconds later they ran out of the lab, closed the door behind them, got into the truck, and headed for the parking lot exit.

When the truck went out of view, Charlaine leapt up on the landing, unlocked the lab door, and pulled it open. She looked immediately to her right, where the doors of the large cabinet were again closed and locked. She cracked the combination lock in about 10 minutes and swung open the double doors. Nothing was left but some stray pieces of plastic and cardboard.

Everything else in the lab looked the same, except to the left of the cabinet, where a pair of Keen shoes caught her eye. She walked around the cabinet and saw the man driving the Mercedes lying with his back propped up against the wall. A tiny hole pierced his chest just below his left shirt pocket, at the top of his heart.

Charlaine thought that he'd probably died instantly. His mouth hung open and his eyes bulged in surprise. Charlaine bent over the hole in the man's shirt and shook her head. She'd never seen such a tidy entrance wound. She stooped low and turned the man over. The bullet, if it was called that, had gone straight through his skin, heart, tissue and bone, leaving an exit wound only slightly larger than the entrance wound on his chest.

Charlaine looked around at the walls and the floor to see if the bullet was embedded somewhere or if a shell had been ejected. On the side wall, about the height of where the man's heart would have been if he was standing at the time of the shooting was a tiny hole, nearly identical to the one in the man's back. The bullet had gone cleanly through the man's body and hit the wall with little disintegration. She thought about trying to dig the projectile from the wall, but it looked deeply embedded, and she didn't want to mess anymore with what was now a crime scene.

Charlaine was far from a ballistics expert, but had seen her share of bullet wounds. She'd never seen anything like this.

48

"No God. No. No. No. No."

Jimmy Chen was repeating it softly, like a prayer, as the panel truck rolled down a largely deserted McComas Street past Port Covington to hook up with I95 then the BW Parkway. Jimmy reached into his jacket pocket and pulled out The Helix prototype, turning it over in his hand as if it was a rare shell he'd found at the beach.

Jimmy had never shot a real gun. Never even thought about it or wanted to. He'd only shot The Helix prototypes to see if they worked, never experiencing the thrill that Colin and Ohtari got out of seeing it tear tiny holes in a heavily padded target backed by a steel plate at the edge of the 3Make parking lot. He'd had no feelings of omnipotence when he fired their invention. He was glad it worked the way Colin had designed it, and that his materials had withstood their testing, but the weapon itself, the firing of it, did nothing special for him. He felt sheepish seeing how animated Colin and Ohtari became after firing the gun. He never thought about what it would do to a living thing, much less a human being standing 10 feet away.

It happened so fast. He hadn't even realized the gun was in his hand. He'd just taken it out of the cabinet and put it in his jacket pocket when Ohtari burst through the door, seething with anger he'd built up after Mikhail's visit; anger that escalated during his drive from Towson to Locust Point.

Jimmy hadn't seen anger like that before. His parents were quiet, demure people. His mother, half Chinese and half American, was an accountant for a large Ford dealership in East Baltimore. His father, first generation from Guangzhou, China, was a programmer for an information security firm in Cockeysville. They never raised their voices to Jimmy or his older sister. Jimmy never played any sports where coaches routinely holler at players. The closest he'd come to seeing this kind of anger was at a Ravens game he'd attended with a high school friend, when the home team lost on a disputed pass interference call.

As Ohtari stood yelling at he and Colin, Jimmy idly fingered the gun grip in his jacket pocket, then pulled it out without thinking, like activating a long-buried human instinct. Despite his nervousness, his hand was steady, aiming the gun just under Ohtari's left breast, just below the bottom of his shirt pocket. Jimmy was marveling at the bold stripe pattern of Ohtari's shirt, how the vertical stripe was perfectly aligned as it ran from the body to the pocket material of the shirt. Craftmanship, thought Jimmy, before Ohtari took a step forward and the gun discharged, sounding like a muted fart. Ohtari dropped immediately, his backside bouncing against the concrete floor and his head ricocheting against the wall. Then he was eerily still, his face crimson with anger.

Colin barely reacted to the shooting. He walked over to Ohtari, stooped in front of him, placed his forearms under Ohtari's armpits and dragged him to the back wall beside the cabinet. There was no conversation as they left the parking lot. But now after the peak of the adrenaline rush was over and they merged into I95 South, Colin looked over at Jimmy and shook his head in pity. Reaching over with his right hand, he gently removed the gun hanging loosely in Jimmy's left hand. He felt suddenly protective toward his...what? Protégé? Colleague? No, friend. Or as close as it comes in Colin's world.

He was far from a martyr, but Colin realized it should have been him with the gun; the guy who'd do practically anything to get his way. Colin had no illusions about his naked ambition: He wanted what he felt he was due. Jimmy just wanted enough money to fuel his dreams.

Colin didn't know what to say. He only talked enough to take care of what he had to take care of. Nothing extraneous. But now he was thinking of Jimmy and what would happen to him. Even if he got out of this he'd likely be hiding the rest of his life. No dream house. No stable of women. No international gaming stardom.

Jimmy's chin sagged on his chest and he was sobbing, the tears rolling down his cheeks and dripping onto his favorite Grayers shirt. Colin reached over to the glove box in front of Jimmy, opened it, and took out a bunch of paper napkins that had accumulated there from fast food visits. He gently placed a few in Jimmy's left hand and raised it to his partner's nose.

"Here, Jimmy, wipe your nose and cheeks. You don't want any snot on your Grayers, homey."

Colin spoke softly, as if to an infant child he wanted to lull asleep.

"We'll be okay. Believe me. This is just a bump. If it ever comes down to it, this was self-defense, pure and simple. There's no crime here, not even in taking the stuff from the lab. We're taking what is ours. What we earned with our brains and hard work. Nobody can take this from us, Jimmy. Not Ohtari or anyone else. Just think: In a couple of months, you'll be exactly where you've wanted to be since you were 10 years old."

It was the longest speech Colin had ever made. Jimmy took a napkin and wiped his cheeks and eyes, then doubled it over and blew his nose into it.

"There you go, Jimbo, there you go," Colin purred. "Nothing like a good nose-blowing to clear the head. We're on our way, homey, on our way."

Jimmy didn't know why, but Colin's words worked. As they rolled down the BW Parkway, the materials and prototypes rattling in the back of the panel truck, Jimmy felt half of a smile blip across his face. Maybe they were on their way to their dreams. Colin hadn't steered them wrong yet.

49

Tony was eyeing a second Miller High Life in the fridge when Charlaine's call came. He knew it was important or she wouldn't call him at home on a Friday night. He just hoped the news wasn't bad.

Charlaine's voice came hard and fast, at almost too much velocity for Tony to comprehend. He told her to slow down and she managed to for about 10 seconds before revving it up again. Tony ran over to his desk and tried to take notes, writing as fast as he could in his version of shorthand.

In their afternoon briefing, Bernard Jamal had given them names and pictures for the possible principals in the case: Bill Christenson, Roland Hines, Colin Barrett, Jimmy Chen, three other engineers working in the nightshift lab, and Spencer Ohtari.

Charlaine had studied the photos intently during the meeting and in the parking lot before entering the 3Make building, so they were embedded in her memory like family portraits.

"White guy was the one called Barrett, the Asian guy was Chen, and the shooting victim was Ohtari."

"Who was the shooter?"

Charlaine shook her head on the other end of the phone.

"If I had to guess, I'd say Barrett. Chen didn't seem to have the disposition for it."

Tony paused and exhaled.

"Yeah, maybe, but those calm, goofy ones can fool you. Remember George Walters?"

Of course she remembered George Walters. The archetypal mild-mannered accountant who carved up his wife Sunny in the bathtub, buried her parts after midnight in various spots of his prolific backyard garden, then reported her missing the next day. He'd of gotten away with it too, had it not been for the neighbor's dog coming home with what turned out to be part of a female femur.

"Whoever it is, we're looking at a felony now Tony. Do you think it's time to call in Baltimore's Finest?"

"I don't know, Goddess. He won't be less dead if we report it, and I don't categorate these two as killers."

"Ohtari might dispute that, Tone, but what do you have in mind?"

"I think we have two plays here: One is seeing where the truck with the GPS tracking—great work on that, by the way—is headed and doing surveillance. The other is paying a visit to the newly minted killers crib to see if they come back there. You got a predilection?"

"I'll go with the truck. I like to finish what I started. You can do the crib detail, but I don't think they're going back there; I think they're officially on the run."

"Geeks on the lam. Should be fun."

"You gotta twisted idea of fun, Tone. One other thing: Should we let Mr. Jamal know?"

"My take is not yet. We gotta lot of preguntas and not enough answers. If it's okay with you, I'd rather see what the rest of the night brings before opening the proverbial kimono."

"Fine with me; I'd definitely like to see your kimono remain closed. But why are you asking for my opinion on all this stuff?"

"All part of the master plan, Goddess. Someday this investigative empire will be yours."

"Don't bullshit me, Tony. You'll be doing this when you have one leg in the grave."

50

What was referred to as the safe house was a circa-1960s ranch house with a barn that was converted into a large garage housing a menagerie of cars, motorcycles, trail bikes, and a few tow trucks. An assorted flock of cars and trucks were strewn across the grounds in various states of living or dying.

The property was at the end of a gravel road called Sylvia Lane. The story goes that the original owner was a fan of the band Dr. Hook's Medicine Show, which had a big hit with "Sylvia's Mother" in the early 70s. In its first incarnation, the property was home to a revolving crew of latent hippies, who cut down some of the trees on the seven-acre property and tried to grow a self-sustaining garden, along with some magic mushrooms, marijuana, and fine whisky distilling in the adjoining woods.

A son of the original owners, Jesse Mattingly, inherited the property, abandoned the straight farming part of the operation, retained the mushroom, weed and distilling operations, and augmented them with a chop shop for stolen vehicles and a repository for weapons of suspicious origins.

Mattingly had none of the high ideals of his parents, but maintained something like a one-big-family atmosphere at the place. In addition to the main house, there were three trailers in various states of disrepair that housed a rotating array of criminals, from weed and oxy dealers to thieves running the gamut from petty shoplifters to those lifting bigger-ticket items such as cars, trucks and jewelry. Everybody from minor grifters to major arms dealers had resided on the property or used Mattingly's services over the past two decades.

Mattingly presided loosely over the operation, smoothing out disputes, casting out perpetual troublemakers and gadflies, and keeping a steady flow of intoxicants and painkillers at the ready. The local cops knew about it, but felt it was above their pay grade to risk their lives by making trouble with the occupants. Besides, Mattingly and his boys, age 37 and 30, contributed heavily to the Fraternal Order of Police and local charities, even sponsoring Mattingly Wreckage baseball and basketball teams. They were also generous with their weed, whisky and oxy for law officers who had a predilection or need for those items. If a cop got in a fix, the Mattinglys were there to help, whether it required offering an alibi, repairing a police or personal car after an illicit accident, or bailing relatives out of jail.

Besides the material items, Mattingly and family offered a prized asset to criminal enterprises: discretion. The only way you developed a relationship with the Mattingly clan was through vetted referrals, and even those wouldn't get you on the inside if you were the kind that liked to mouth off at bars or simply rubbed Jesse the wrong way. Jesse and his sons would treat their guests, colleagues and partners like family, unless you fucked up or showed signs of disloyalty.

Mikhail, Brad and Jesse were sitting on the front porch with fresh beers and a cooler promising more. A smoker in the yard, built from an old propane tank, sent up smoke from pork shoulders Jesse had slow cooking for the last 12 hours. Between the smoke and chill in the air, the night was blissfully free of mosquitoes. Jesse didn't know what Mikhail and Brad did but he liked them. They were both solid dudes. Mikhail paid in cash and didn't try to bullshit him.

The three men were talking fishing when the sound of tires on gravel echoed through the woods. Jesse casually reached in back of him and pulled his AR-15 loaded with hollow-body bullets onto his lap. Mikhail looked at his watch, thinking it should be Barrett and Chen, but not declaring anything until the front end of the panel truck came into view. Jesse immediately relaxed and returned the rifle to its place leaning against the front wall of the house. Mikhail got up and walked down the two front steps of the porch into the gravel-filled clearing that served as a parking area.

Barrett was the first to get out, jumping out of the truck and walking briskly toward Mikhail. Chen followed, walking slowly with his head down. Mikhail signaled them to the back of the truck, not wanting Jesse to hear the conversation. He trusted him, but Mikhail always operated on a need-to-know basis and Jesse, no matter how reliable, didn't need to know anything about their operation.

As Mikhail drew closer to Barrett, he saw an uncharacteristic look on his face. Something like confusion or dismay, his lips pursed and his eyes wide. Chen kept his eyes on the gravel. Barrett always took the lead for Chen, even though Chen was older and more articulate.

Mikhail halted about three feet away from Barrett and tried to keep it casual.

"Copacetic?" he asked quietly.

"Almost," Barrett whispered.

"I take it 'almost' means no," said Mikhail softly.

"Yes...I mean no...it didn't go as planned." Barrett paused to wipe his mouth and clear his throat. "Everything's out of the lab, but there's a...an...a...complication."

Mikhail moved closer to Barrett and kept his voice barely above a whisper. "You're among friends, Colin. Tell me. Take your time. Breathe."

"It...it...was Ohtari. He showed up as we were loading the truck. He was yelling and screaming. Getting in our face."

"And?"

"Jimmy. He had a Helix in his hand. It went off. Hit Ohtari in the chest. He's gone."

Mikhail smiled and it sent a full-body chill through Barrett and Chen.

"Well, well. I didn't take Jimmy C. for a killer."

Barrett shook his head and waved his right hand in front of his face as if chasing away a bee.

"No, no way. He just reacted. Like instinct."

Mikhail smiled again.

"Well, you never know what's inside a man or woman until you apply pressure. The body?"

"We left it in the lab," Barrett answered shakily.

"Anyone likely to find it there, in say, the next few hours?"

Barrett shook his head. He and Chen had decided during the drive not to mention the cleaning lady.

"No, don't think so. Look, Mikhail, I'm sorry...we did our best."

"No need to apologize, Colin. You probably did me a favor. Did you get all the stuff from the lab and do you have all the design files?"

Barrett nodded.

"Then you boys did your job. Come on, let's have a beer. Jesse says his signature barbecue will be ready in about 15 minutes and he has all the sides prepared. We'll have ourselves a little celebration."

Chen kept his eyes on the ground and shook his head. Mikhail walked around Barrett, patted him on the shoulder, put his other arm around Chen and pulled him forward beside him and Barrett. They looked like three teammates leaving the field after a game, united in victory or defeat. It was hard to tell which.

51

Mikhail and Brad weren't staying overnight at the Mattingly compound. Each wanted to be alone at their respective hotels for the night. Brad wanted to return home to the Tidewater area, but Mikhail had asked him to stay on for another day, "just in case." Brad was still feeling uneasy about his day's work, but didn't want to turn down another good paying job if it was convenient and timely. Mikhail didn't have anything specifically in mind for Brad, but the way things were developing he wanted to have him on immediate call in the Baltimore area.

Barrett and Chen would stay the night at the main safe house. Mikhail had a plan to get them out of the country within the next few days, but meanwhile thought they were safe at Mattingly's place. He had already dispatched two guys—the same ones who did the work at Bill Christenson's house to make it look like he'd skipped town—to 3Make headquarters to dispose of Spencer Ohtari's body. Mikhail gave no specific instructions on what to do with Ohtari; he just wanted them to make the body disappear someplace where it wouldn't be discovered for anywhere from a few weeks to...well, forever.

Mikhail didn't worry much about Barrett. The guy was a bit like himself. A loner who didn't need to talk to anyone, nor cared enough about anyone for feelings to get in the way. Chen was a different story. He still saw his family and had some party buddies with whom he was relatively close. He also liked weed, which Mikhail loathed. People talked when they did weed or when they drank heavily. He hadn't worried much about it before because Barrett was always at Chen's side and Chen, despite his social nature, was never interested in talking about his work. Barrett, like Mikhail, could fade into the woodwork almost anywhere. Not so for Chen.

It wasn't in Mikhail's nature to be angry with Chen. The guy wasn't built for the situation he ended up in. If anything, Mikhail was upset at himself for not having Ohtari shadowed after he'd delivered the ultimatum. Just like Ohtari to put a wrench in the works. Mikhail should have known he wouldn't bow out easily. At least it happened when no one was around and the weekend bought Mikhail and his team some time.

Mikhail would have to step lightly around the Chen situation. The Helix prototypes worked as designed and the materials held up well in initial testing, but there had been no time for durability tests. They didn't know if the materials would hold up under mass additive manufacturing of hundreds of units per machine each day. Or if they would continue to perform over hundreds or thousands of shots. If there were any adjustments needed from the material side of things, they would need Chen's skills and knowledge. There were reasons that they chose Chen and were willing to pay him millions for his developmental work and continued input as they scaled production worldwide.

Mikhail thought again about Roland Hines. He was the perpetually curious sort from what Mikhail knew. The kind of guy unlikely to take the resignations of Barrett and Chen and the disappearance of Christenson at face value. The tap on Hines' phone was still working and through the GPS they could keep track of his whereabouts. Fortunately, Hines was still at his beach place and wasn't expected in Baltimore until Monday. Mikhail didn't know if Hines was aware of the cabinet in the nightshift lab belonging to Barrett and Chen, but he'd no doubt become suspicious to find it empty. Hines' first assumption, Mikhail surmised, would be the correct one; that Barrett and Chen had skipped off with proprietary 3Make technologies, tools and materials.

The other possible ball in the air was Brad Davenport. Brad was never forthcoming, but he seemed more reticent than usual to discuss his job that afternoon. He shrugged off Mikhail's attempts to pry any details from him, saying the fewer who knew the better. Mikhail didn't pursue it. As long as it didn't impinge on the overall operation, Mikhail didn't press people on how they got things done.

As he pulled into the hotel parking lot near BWI Airport, Mikhail started to relax a bit. He could access his room without going through the lobby. Once inside, he'd be alone. He would have a three-finger hit of scotch, look out the window while Mingus played on his headset, and calmly think through today and what's ahead for the rest of the weekend. He'd move the pieces around in his head like a chessboard. Get a good night's sleep. He always welcomed the coming of a new day.

Unlike Ohtari, Mikhail knew there was a lot of hard strategic work ahead, leading to the possibility of more missteps. No time for celebration. No back patting. Just stay the course. For a guy like Mikhail, everything was a work in progress. Obstacles wait around the corner to ambush you. The best you could do was anticipate and react with calmness, swiftness and rationality.

52

Charlaine stopped on the narrow shoulder of a two-lane highway snaking through the woods. According to the GPS signal, the panel truck was a half mile down a gravel road about 50 yards ahead. She got out of the Forester and looked around to see if anyone was watching.

After she discovered Ohtari's body, she'd briefly thought about hopping into his car to follow Barrett and Chen. She'd decided to stick with her car, as it had the stuff she needed for a stakeout. She hated stakeouts, especially ones that involved being outdoors. She was a city girl. She'd been to a couple of summer camps when she was a child, but hadn't enjoyed them. The mosquitoes at night. Smoky-smelling clothes from campfires. The hard ground and leaky tent when it rained. Swimming in water teeming with sea nettles.

Her grandmother had always stressed the importance of having a roof over her family's heads, no matter how flimsy. It's what separates us from the animal world, she said. Charlaine was proud that she owned a house and wasn't subject to a landlord's control. She made her mortgage payment each month on time, sometimes doubling up on monthly payments if cash flow was strong. Joy felt the same and Charlaine likely wouldn't have pursued the relationship further if she didn't. A home was so important to Charlaine that she rarely wanted to be away from it.

Charlaine went to the back of the Forester, pulled out bug spray and coated the exposed parts of her body. She pulled her socks overtop of the cuffs of her gray sweats and put on a black hooded jacket. Fortunately, it wasn't too hot or cold and didn't look like rain. She grabbed a couple of granola bars and a water bottle that she hung from a clip on her waist. She pulled out a torn t-shirt from the back seat and tied it to the driver's side door handle. Once again the slightly disreputable look of the Forester, with dings, scrapes and a dent in the back fender, presented a good facsimile of a car that might break down. Charlaine knew that all the important parts of the car, those unseen by the casual eye, were in perfect working order.

As she walked toward the gravel road, Charlaine scanned the surrounding trees to see if there were any signs of video cameras or motion sensors. She'd prefer to walk on the side of the road if possible, as there was little or no shoulder and thick underbrush on either side of the road clearing. Her steps were long, but light, barely registering on the gravel. There was a quarter-moon out so there was some light, but not much, as the trees cast much of the road in shadows.

About a quarter mile in, she heard the unmistakable sound of car tires crunching on gravel. She jumped off the road, landing in a gulley with about a half-inch of muddied water pooled at the bottom. She felt the water seep through her sweats just as headlights swept over the top of her head.

Two vehicles. From what she could see the first was a midsize sedan, probably a Camry, followed by a Ford truck pulling a trailer with a newish-looking fishing boat. She didn't rise from the murk until she couldn't be seen in the truck's rearview mirror.

Once the vehicles went around the bend and out of sight, Charlaine perked her ears for any other sounds, picked herself up from the gulley and climbed back to the road, the right side of her body soaked in mud. "Fresh hell in laundering" was Joy's go-to phrase when Charlaine presented her with clothing studded with briars, streaked with grease, or reeking of dog shit. "A thousand stories in the naked city" was Charlaine's stock reply.

As she continued up the road, Charlaine got quieter, taking long strides and lightly landing her feet like a praying mantis climbing the stem of a plant. When she showed the technique at home Joy said she looked like John Cleese in the Monty Python Ministry of Silly Walks skit. Charlaine googled it later that night and had to laugh at the connection.

Charlaine couldn't figure out why her instincts drove her to think of funny or silly things when she was in these situations. She figured it was some kind of relief mechanism, like steam escaping when a valve is loosened. Whatever the explanation, the brief moment of levity was followed by a wave of calmness.

As she rounded a turn, the side of a brick ranch house appeared and the road ended in a driveway to the back of the house. Edging around the tree line on the side of the road, Charlaine took in the scene. Typical suburban rancher on a big plot of property, with a barn-like garage that was bigger than the house. She continued around the tree line, watching for any dogs that might be guarding the property. She saw no movement nor heard any noise outside except for the rhythmic chirping of insects. The smell of smoking meat hung in the air and Charlaine shuddered with hunger.

Several lights were on in the house and she heard the bass and booms from a movie or game seeping through the walls. She made her way from tree to tree along the side of the house toward the back, where a screened-in porch spanned the length of the back wall. The porch was dark, but at the far end Charlaine could see the faint glow of a screen and the silhouette of a person wearing headphones. She looked toward the back of the yard and saw the front of the panel truck pulled up against the back door of the garage. The truck was mostly concealed from the house by the garage, unless the headphone wearer decided to migrate to the other side of the porch.

53

Jimmy Chen was a partier uncomfortable in conventional social settings. He was fine where there was music, loud conversation, and drinks flowing, or within a multi-player online gaming situation. But put him at a dinner table, at a company gathering, or even a casual lounging around with people he didn't know and he was struck mute, as he was now sitting with a plate of barbecue and sides with Jesse Mattingly, his sons, Colin, and a few assorted women with official or unofficial attachments to the Mattingly family.

He was thinking about Mikhail. There was a coldness in his eyes, a smile that wasn't quite a smile, that chilled Jimmy from his head to his feet. He was still shivering, although the den in which they were seated was a perfectly comfortable 72 degrees.

Normally, Jimmy would have been cruising the bars and clubs in the city, trying to score. He didn't score that often because of the competition. There were always more loose men than women prowling on a Friday night. Friday was renowned as a singles night, whether you were actually single or not. Attachments tended to wash away under the strobe lights or heavy lubrication of a Friday night. Right now, Jimmy would do anything to lose himself in the music and the swaying hips of a woman in a tight-fitting skirt. Sitting here in the den was almost like the obligatory visits to his parents' house for holidays and special occasions. He thought he loved them and his sister, but wasn't too certain. Anything bordering on emotional terrain made him hesitant and doubtful.

He got up from the easy chair, went to the kitchen, threw away his paper plate, and walked down the hall to the back porch, where two daybeds had been set up for him and Colin. A phrase was running through his head: *This changes everything*. He remembered hearing people say that after 9/11. He also remembered his father, thinking Jimmy was out of hearing distance, saying to his mother as they cleared the dinner table, "This changes nothing, except people of Middle Eastern descent will bear the brunt of it. They'll be profiled, discriminated against, beaten up in certain neighborhoods." Then Jimmy and his parents started seeing it happen all over again with Covid, except this time it was against people who looked like him and his father. His mother and sister, whose facial features leaned toward Anglo, were on safer ground.

This changes everything. It rang through his head the whole ride to the safe house from 3Make. Colin had done his best to calm him and it was almost endearing. But Jimmy knew the extent of Colin's emotional depth, and was pretty certain he'd used up his reserves on the drive to this house in the woods. The people staying in the house seemed nice enough, but they were country people in Jimmy's eyes, the kind of people his father warned him about. "They might act friendly, but stay aware. Racism can rear its head at any time."

Jimmy had never felt so unsettled. He didn't normally think about his future, except for what was immediately ahead of him within the next few days or weeks at the most. The whole prospect of developing The Helix and the aftermath was a fantasy, but one that was becoming real as they got closer to the finish line. He had given himself the luxury of thinking he'd party tonight, once they'd turned in their resignations, downloaded the design files to the Russian servers, cleared the cabinet of the materials and prototypes, and returned the panel truck to the safe house.

The shooting changed that. Mikhail told Jimmy and Colin to stay at the house, destroy their phones, and communicate with no one until arrangements could be made to take them to a safer locale. If it had just been taking the materials and prototypes from 3Make, he and Colin were unlikely to be pursued. After all, 3Make would feel a fair share of embarrassment for allowing The Helix operation to take place on company property and even benignly sanctioning it. 3Make was more likely to sweep it under the rug and try to minimize the damage, much like what was done with Ohtari at Sintology. Jimmy would likely never be able to work in the 3D printing industry again, unless it was under a new identity in another country, but at least he wouldn't have been a fugitive.

Jimmy was exhausted as his emotions swung from sadness to panic to regret to anger. When he closed his eyes, he saw the small spot appear on Ohtari's shirt, the jerking of his upper body, neck and head, the splatter of the concrete block wall when hit by the bullet that had ripped through Ohtari's body. Sometimes the scene was silent and other times Jimmy heard the crack of Ohtari's butt against the hard lab floor. It all happened in a second, but Jimmy's mind played it back in slow motion, ending with Ohtari's face frozen in stunned surprise.

Except for the underlying buzz of insects, the porch was quiet. But inside Jimmy's head, the walls were closing in, and the pounding, like a small tom-tom at first, was escalating to kettle drum proportions. He pulled out his laptop, put on his headphones, and tried to quell the uprising with a Yung Lean mixtape. But even that reliable palliative failed to engage him. He thought about asking Jesse or his sons if they had some weed, but was afraid that they might report him to Mikhail, whom Jimmy knew disdained weed and other types of mind-altering substances.

Jimmy needed something to take him away. He'd never get to sleep otherwise. Then he remembered that stash of Thai stick he'd scored a few weeks ago. He'd not cracked it because he still had a few grams of Columbian. He'd left the stash at his apartment, thinking he'd go back there and pack his stuff tonight after they'd loaded the panel truck. He'd also left behind his customized game controller, 3D-printed to fit perfectly in his hands, and some of his favorite pieces of apparel. Now, under Mikhail's orders he won't be able to go back to the apartment. The thought of never having that controller in his hands, never tasting that opium-laden Thai stick or wearing his favorite shirts and jeans, sent Jimmy dipping helplessly toward depression.

54

Charlaine estimated that it was 30 yards between where she was standing on the edge of the woods to where the panel truck was parked behind the garage. In between was open space across a weed-filled patch of earth, then the gravel road to the back of the garage.

Taking a final look at the house, she made her move. Her sneakers hitting the gravel sounded abnormally loud to her, like a series of small explosions. She hoped that the people in the house still had the sound cranked up on the TV or video game console and the person on the porch was still wearing headphones.

Charlaine ducked out of sight behind the truck and edged around to the driver's side, opening the door as quietly as she could and leaving it open as she crawled into the front seat. She switched off the light on the ceiling of the cab and looked around for a key. First in the ignition, then in the visor over the windshield, then the glove compartment and under the seat. Nothing, but she always checked.

She climbed out of the truck cab, closed the door as gently as possible, and walked to the back of the truck, debating whether she should open the rolling door a little at a time or in one big movement. She decided to open it all at once. It sounded like thunder, but when it was over, she looked back at the house and saw no lights go on or any movement outside. She waited about a minute to make sure no one was stirring and then climbed inside the truck bed, rolling down the door behind her.

She turned on her phone light and scanned the boxes lined up along the walls of the truck. Much the same as she saw in the lab: A box of bottles labeled as different types of resins. Spools of what looked like plastic-coated wires. A couple of boxes that felt like granular laundry detergent when she lifted them.

But then there were items she hadn't seen in the nightshift lab: A box with about a dozen flat batteries like those used in a digital camera. She grabbed one of these from the box and shoved it into the pocket of her sweats. A box sitting by itself in the corner contained something extraordinary: Several outer-space-looking handguns barely larger than a kid's squirt gun and nearly as light, with what looked like a chamber of ever-widening circles, like a snail shell. The guns looked identical until Charlaine took a closer look and saw slight variances in size and shape. Below the handguns were several small boxes of what she suspected was ammunition, but the bullets—if you could call them that—were non-metal with no casings. They were about an inch and a half long and the diameter of a fork tine.

She picked up one of the guns and hefted it in her palm. It didn't appear to be metal, but not like any kind of plastic she'd seen either. When she picked up the presumed ammo it was razor sharp at one end, like the tip of a large needle. Rolling two of the bullets in her palm, she flashed on the wound in Ohtari's chest. Same diameter.

How could you propel something that small and light with enough velocity to go cleanly through a man's chest, straight through his heart and out his back with a hole nearly the same size and definition as the one in the front?

Charlaine had seen ghost guns. They were blocky plastic things that looked untrustworthy. She'd never fired one and didn't intend to, valuing her right hand and the rest of her body. She'd read somewhere that the incidences of ghost gun misfires and explosions were very high, but most went unreported for obvious reasons. Still, people continued to buy the guns because they were cheap and untraceable. She'd read that Baltimore City police had recovered more than 350 ghost guns last year, an increase of 1,000 percent from two years ago. Despite the risks, business was booming.

What were these guys doing? Using 3Make's facilities to develop a new generation of ghost gun? Did they have a formula and plan for somehow mass producing these things? It made Charlaine shudder. But it also made her smile, because she now had evidence, and if they could do a search of Barrett's and Chen's laptops they just might find incriminating design and manufacturing files.

Charlaine stuck one of the guns and several pieces of ammo into her jacket pockets and started walking toward the rolling door when she heard footsteps outside. She froze and waited a moment until she heard the driver's side door of the truck slam closed and the sound of the engine shaking to a start. She leaped toward the door and was thrown backwards as the truck backed up abruptly. She struggled to stand up, but fell for a second time as the truck thrust forward.

She rose to her knees and then to her feet, taking deep breaths to clear her head. The truck was moving slowly along the gravel road. She tried to visualize how far they had traveled. When the truck started turning left, she figured they were at the first bend, about 200 yards from the house. She moved toward the rolling door, lifted it up and closed it behind her, stooping on the edge of the bumper. When the truck slowed near the end of the road, she jumped off the back into the gravel, flexing her knees to minimize the impact. She scampered into the woods opposite the passenger side of the truck. The driver paused at the stop sign and made a right-hand turn onto the two-lane highway. Charlaine managed to get a glimpse of the driver: It was Jimmy Chen.

Charlaine sprinted toward her car to follow the truck when she remembered the GPS device in the wheel well. She almost laughed as she exhaled in relief and heard her late father's voice saying, "Easy greasy, you have a long way to slide."

55

"Turn that shit down. Now!"

Jesse Mattingly heard the sound of gravel crunching on the driveway and looked out the front window of his house. The panel truck was leaving the property. He couldn't tell who was at the wheel but assumed it was one of those Mikhail guys; the guys he was supposed to be looking after. He told Mikhail he wasn't no babysitter. Mikhail just shrugged and said that they wouldn't be going anywhere. This was exactly why Jesse didn't want to get involved in his clients' dealings. He'd offer his services, but didn't need or want to know the specifics of their operations.

Jesse ran to the kitchen and found one of the two guys, the white one named Colin, peering out of the window with a stricken look on his face.

"That your boy in that truck?" Jesse asked, seemingly casual but with an edge that Colin detected.

Colin turned from the window, looking surprised.

"I don't know. I thought he was on the porch." Colin knew he sounded lame. He couldn't lie worth a shit. Jesse shook his head.

"Y'all still had the keys, so who else could it be? I distinctly heard Mikhail tell y'all not to go nowhere. I don't know what you got in that truck, but it shouldn't be parading around on the streets. I'm gonna give Mikhail a call."

Jesse reached in his back pocket for his phone as Colin rushed forward and grabbed his arm.

"Please...don't do that. I...I think I know where he's going. I'd call him but we don't have phones anymore. I have my car here. I'll catch up to him and make sure he gets back here safe and sound."

Jesse shook his head.

"No offense, but I don't care whether he gets back here safe and sound. That's between you, if you're his brah, and Mikhail. But that's my truck and Mikhail has a, whatchacallit, vested interest in what's inside. Right now, it looks like that Chinese boy is stealing from both of us."

Colin shook his head back and forth rapidly.

"He wouldn't do anything like that. I know where he's going. Give me two hours, okay?"

"Two hours for what?"

"Two hours and I'll have the truck back to you, with everything in the back. We didn't come this far to do something stupid. Mikhail doesn't need to know about this."

"I'll be the one to decide that. How do I know both of you won't take off?"

That's when Colin thought about the cash, the $2,000 in hundreds that Mikhail had given both he and Jimmy, calling it "walkaround cash, just in case."

"How about if you hold onto some cash...uh, a thousand bucks...until we get back?"

Jesse paused for about 10 seconds, looking Colin straight in the eye. Sweat dripped from Colin's armpits.

"I don't know why I'd do this, but I'm going to trust you this once. But not for nothing. I'll trust you for that thousand and you won't be seeing it returned."

Colin nodded his head in relief.

"Alright, alright, you won't be sorry, Sir."

"Don't sir me. Just make sure you get my truck and Mikhail's goods back here in two hours or you and your boy will wish you'd never set eyes on me or my sons."

"Yes, Sir, I mean, yes Mr. Mattingly."

Colin turned to walk away when Jesse grabbed his arm.

"Not so fast. You don't think I'd let you go alone do you? You think I'm stupid? My boy John will be escorting you for this here trip. And there'll be hell to pay if you ain't both back in two hours."

Jesse kept a hold on Colin's arm and perp-walked him into the living room.

"John. Colin here thinks he knows where his bro is going with our truck. I want you to ah, accompany him on his search."

John cast his eyes on the floor, let out his breath, and gently placed the paperback he was holding on an end table.

"This better be good, dude," he said to Colin, eyeing him up like an undersized fish that he needed to throw back. "I was just hitting the good part."

56

J immy Chen was lost.

He had no sense of direction. Why would he? Why bother when there are Google Maps and Waze? Knowing where's north, south, east or west might be good for people hiking in the woods or desert but what practical application did it have in the real world? It's like those people who think they are smart because they can do cursive writing or long division in their heads.

But now Jimmy was driving a truck for the first time and without a phone. He knew that he was south of the city, but had no idea how to get to the apartment from here. He hadn't paid attention when Colin drove the truck to the safe house from 3Make. Why would he?

It was dark on these back roads and you couldn't see a sign until you were right on top of it. The signs didn't help much anyway because Jimmy had never heard of any of these places. What is Lothian? Or Harwood? Or Davidsonville? Why would he ever go to any of these places? Why would anyone want to live there?

Jimmy's purview was Baltimore City and County. Maybe DC once in a while. He could get to a few places by memory, like 3Make from his apartment or from his apartment to some of the clubs he visited frequently or maybe to GameStop. To him, knowing geography was a waste of good brain cells.

His face was getting hot and his hands had a death grip on the steering wheel. His arms shook. He let out a scream that scared him. Jimmy never knew any trauma until tonight. Now it was escalating in a bad way, like shitty code that fucks up everything that comes after it. He just wanted to get back to the apartment. Get his controller. Get the rest of that Columbian and Thai stick. Pick up some of his favorite clothes. *Please help me, God.*

Jimmy shook his head at the improbability of appealing to a God he never believed in. His father and mother never went to church. They referenced God occasionally when he was growing up, but only in the way other people their age and social status did. Jimmy used to laugh to himself when his father would say to someone "God bless you." It was part of what Jimmy saw as his father's over-striving act. Trying to be a good American. His mother came by it more naturally, but even she sounded off key to Jimmy when she summoned God, unless she shouted "goddammit" when she dropped a dish or couldn't find her keys.

If he got out of this, Jimmy might learn how to read a map. And maybe he'd pray once in a while—not just when he was in trouble, but to praise the Lord, however you do that. Just let him find a sign that directs him to Baltimore, then maybe to Parkville. If he got to Parkville, he could find Harford Rd. and then his apartment building. He wasn't that pitiful. Or he could pull into a gas station and ask directions. As long as nobody pulled that east/west north/south stuff on him.

C'mon, c'mon. Where is a Baltimore sign? Don't these people go to Baltimore? Don't they go to an O's or Ravens game, to a restaurant in the city, to see a show at the Hippodrome? What do they do with themselves? Maybe they're like Colin, who seemingly needed no entertainment. What sad lives! No wonder he wanted out of here. Bangkok or Hanoi or Kuala Lumpur, those were the kind of places he wanted. Non-stop action. He'd never been to any of those places, but had seen the videos and heard the stories.

He came to a stop at an intersection with a sign indicating to the right was Annapolis and to the left was Crownsville. He'd heard of Annapolis, but not Crownsville. Then he saw an arrow with an airplane icon on it pointing in the direction of Crownsville.

He took the left, heading up Rt. 450 to 97 North. *Ah, north, north is good.* Then another thought. He had $2,000 in his pocket, a Visa card with $25,000 worth of credit, and access to $350,000 or so in his bank account. Why not find a hotel for a night, book a flight to Bangkok and get away from all this? Just disappear and start over. But first, get that controller and the weed. Everything else will fall into place. It always did for Jimmy, somehow or another.

57

"Hey, Tone. Just a heads up that Jimmy Chen might be coming your way."

Charlaine was calling from the car as she monitored the GPS tracking of the panel truck. Chen was taking a meandering path to wherever he was heading and she would soon catch up with him. Might as well tail him, she thought.

"Yeah, I'm monitoring the GPS too. How do you know he's coming here? Dude's like Dion: the wanderer."

"Deion Sanders?"

"Dion DiMucci, the legend! You never heard of him? 'Oh well I'm the type of guy who will never settle down, where pretty girls are well, you know that I'm around'..."

"Okay, Tone, cut the shit. You don't pay me enough to listen to you sing."

"Lidia says I sing like Dean Martin."

"Dean Martin?"

"Fahgettaboutit. Why do ya think he's coming this way?"

"Don't know. Just a hunch. I don't know where else he'd go, unless he's delivering the goods in the truck, which I don't think they'd let him do."

"Who's they?"

"That's the billion-dollar question, Tone. There were people in the house, but I didn't get to see them. I was only there a short time when

Chen came out to the truck. Almost caught me snooping around in back of it."

"What's he carrying in that truck?"

"A lot of stuff I don't recognize, but I got it all on video. We can show it to Roland or someone else at 3Make and they can probably ID it. There were a few things I definitely recognized and I escaped with some evidence."

"What things?"

"A ghost gun like I've never seen before, with ammo I've never seen before, and what looks like a battery pack that slips into the grip. This is what was used to off Ohtari. The bullet went straight through him, back out the other side and into a cinder block wall behind him. Bullets are really small, so must have been propelled at a high velocity to do that kind of damage."

Tony let out a low whistle.

"Whatta ya think we're into here, Goddess?"

"I think Barrett, Chen and maybe Ohtari were developing some kind of super ghost gun, Tone. Something went down between Barrett, Chen and Ohtari. Ohtari lost."

"Is Barrett in the car with Chen?"

"No. Chen's alone."

"You don't think Chen's trying a getaway do you?"

"I don't think he's got the balls for it, but you know what you always say."

"Yeah, assume nothing and suspect everything."

"Exactly. I don't know who those people in the house are, but you might want to see if some of the local AA County boys in blue can check them out. Barrett might still be there. This thing is starting to look like a lot more than two nerds fucking around."

"I agree with your perspicaciousness, Goddess. I know some blues in AA County who owe me chips. I'll see if I can get them over there. I'm assuming these guys will be armed?"

"I think you can count on that, Tone. I just hope they don't have any more of those guns like the ones in the truck. There are only about a dozen in there, all a bit different, so maybe they're protos. By the looks of Ohtari, they're in working order. Scary prospect if they can be mass-produced with 3D printing. You think we should get some law over to 3Make to process that body?"

"I still say hold off, Goddess. I'd like to give them a nice tidy package."

"Okay, boss, but I don't think this shit was ever tidy."

"Me either, but I can only hope. At the very least, maybe we can brace Chen and get him to tell us what went down with Ohtari."

"Yeah, the way he's driving he'll run outta gas before he gets where he's going. Then I can pick him up and grill his nerdy ass."

"We might have to bring Jacey in as an interpreter. You know, to translate tech speak into good ole American English."

"I always wondered what you spoke, Tony. Oh shit, where's this guy going now? Hope you got plenty of coffee. This could be a long night."

"Why they pay us the big bucks."

"Speak for yourself."

58

"Dude, where you going? The car's this way."

John Mattingly pointed to the opposite side of the parking pad from where Colin was heading.

"I was going to drive."

"Naw, doesn't work that way. I drive and you give me directions. I don't know you well enough to sit in a car that you're driving. You could end up being like Christopher Walken in 'Annie Hall'."

"Who's Christopher Walken and what's Annie Hall?"

"Damn, it's going to be a long two hours. Now where to, Colin?"

"Parkville, it's north of the city."

"I know Parkville, dude. We kicked their asses in the state lax finals."

Colin moved a pile of books from the passenger seat and placed them on the back seat, which was strewn with hardcover and paperback books. John put the car in gear and accelerated out of the driveway into the gravel road. When they entered the highway, John glanced at Colin.

"So, why Parkville?"

"Our apartment."

"Why do you think he's going there?"

"Just think he will."

"Why?"

"Just think so."

John shook his head slowly back and forth and wagged his index finger at Colin.

"Listen, Colin. You might want to be more forthcoming with me, okay? I'm one of the good ones. You're lucky you didn't get my older brother. He'd liable to carve a new one for you. Me, I'm more of the amiable type. I help old ladies get toilet paper off the top shelf of the grocery store. I stop my car for squirrels crossing the street. I donate time to Habitat for Humanity. So be thankful for small favors. Again: Why do you think your friend is going back to your apartment?"

"He's not my friend."

"Okay, whatever, that's your business. I repeat the question."

"Probably to get his game controller and some weed."

"Hmmm. Why didn't he just ask about the weed? Not my preferred intoxicant, but it's readily available to us. What's so special about the controller?"

Colin shifted in his seat and felt a trail of sweat run down the back of his neck.

"Mikhail doesn't like weed, so Jimmy wouldn't ask. The controller is custom-made to fit Jimmy's hands."

"He's a serious gamer?"

"Yeah."

"Is he any good?"

"I guess so. I don't pay attention to it."

John raised his eyebrows.

"Just what do you pay attention to Colin? What are you guys into anyway? What's in that van?"

Colin shook his head rapidly back and forth.

"I can't tell you that. I can't tell anyone that."

"Okay, I can respect that. I'm not trying to make you snitch or anything."

"I'm no snitch!"

John reached over and patted Colin on the shoulder. Colin flinched.

"Easy, man. Why so jumpy?"

"No reason. It's been a long day."

John nodded his head and replied in a soft, reassuring voice.

"Okay, just relax. Push the seat back and lean your head on that headrest. But, you will tell me when we get near your apartment. Your secret will be safe with me, but I'll need to know in case I have to decide whether to put my neck on the line or not. Do you understand that, Colin?"

Colin shook his head up and down like a bobble-head doll.

Five minutes later, as John merged into 97, Colin was asleep against the window, looking peaceful, angelic even. He looked younger than John, like one of those Orioles bonus babies that John sometimes went to see play in Bowie. John's father told him that Colin and the Asian guy, Jimmy, were some kind of tech geniuses. He didn't know the nature of their genius, just that they could deliver something for which Mikhail and his people placed great value.

John wondered why those two guys would get involved with whatever they were involved in. From everything he'd read, those tech guys, the good ones, could make millions within a decade or less. Why not just stay on the straight and narrow and retire when you're 40? Buy a big plot of land somewhere nice, like in the mountains or on the beach. Toes in the sand or kayaking a pristine lake.

John couldn't understand people motivated purely by money, as he assumed Colin and Jimmy were. He was in the family business but not wedded to it like his father and older brother. He didn't know what they got out of it. Sure, they had money and a certain amount of clout in the community, but the work itself was boring and repetitious. They were basically a service company, giving people what they couldn't easily acquire elsewhere at a fair price. Drugs, cars, trucks, weapons, loans, lodging free of prying eyes.

His father and brother were pragmatic and simple, where John was a dreamer. The books were a way to channel those dreams and explore new ones. They transported John from his everyday life to places that made his mind and heart race. The only value he placed on money is that it might buy him freedom somewhere down the line. He'd finally have a chance to find out what he might have been had he not been co-opted into the family business by the time he was 16. Up until then, he thought he might be a librarian or a sportswriter or maybe even a musician—his mother had played guitar until the cancer got her and told John when he was nine that he had the touch. He liked the idea of having something unique to him; something that his brother Stephen didn't have.

John looked over at Colin, wondering if that's why he and Jimmy were doing whatever they were doing. Maybe it wasn't for money. Maybe it was for the thrill of doing something nobody else has done. John had seen all kinds of criminals. People think their motivations are simple. But to John's eyes they rarely are. Only one thing never changed: A significant number were in it for the kicks. Money was just the propellant.

59

Jimmy Chen thought he might have his bearings as he approached BWI Airport on Rt. 100 and saw the sign for 295 toward Baltimore. He noted the signs for local hotels, figuring he'd come back here after picking up the controller, weed and clothes. He also remembered a phone stored in a box of old computer and electrical parts in the back of his bedroom closet.

Jimmy thought about letting Colin know where he planned to leave the truck, but he didn't know how to contact him. He had his number stored in the old phone, but Colin was supposed to destroy his phone too. Jimmy hoped that Colin wouldn't be held responsible for whatever he did, but he didn't feel like he owed Colin anything. Or anybody anything. He smiled at the notion of his family and his acquaintances not knowing where he was. Jimmy Chen, man of mystery.

Jimmy was always a good kid. He was taught to take advantage of the opportunities he had and others didn't. It was drilled into him since he was five how fortunate he was; what it would have been like if he'd grown up in China. But, he knew plenty of Chinese men and women who'd stayed in the states after college and they weren't any different than him. They didn't particularly honor where they came from or stay forever beholden to the sacrifices of their parents. In many ways, they were as self-centered as he was, always striving for something. Status, maybe. Wealth. Raising the perfect American family. All the American dream stuff was alive within them.

The fact that Jimmy was not fully Chinese didn't matter. Didn't matter to the Census Bureau. Didn't matter to the tough kids in high school, who put post-it notes on his locker with "CHINK" scrawled on them. When Covid came around, he was regularly eyeballed in clubs and the grocery store. Even at 3Make, which was the most diverse environment Jimmy had ever been in, there were signs of wariness. The three Chinese engineers in the company tended to sit together in the in-house café, and when Covid started spreading, other employees gave their table a wide berth, sitting even farther away than the recommended six feet. One old engineer asked Jimmy what he knew about the lab in Wuhan, as if he had some kind of inside intelligence.

He wouldn't miss any of them. And he didn't care whether they missed him or not. Once he got on that airplane, he could be anybody. His ticket and passport might read "James Chen" but no one would know him. He could be Bill Smith. Somchai Chen. Bao Wang. He'd be a foreigner everywhere he traveled and it wouldn't matter. He'd take on a new name in Thailand. Poof, Jimmy Chen as dead as a house mouse.

He'd have to think up a new gaming handle. He'd called himself "Posh" for most of his gaming life, but that would change too. He thought it was a cool handle, but he loved the idea of reinventing himself. He'd get a new avatar too. With the $350K he'd saved he'd get himself into a nice crib, buy a new gaming rig, big 4K screen, and a little furniture. Then he'd carry out his plan to dominate the Dota 2 universe, scooping up a chunk of that $30 million in tournament money. Nobody would know who he was in real life, just the GOAT who came out of nowhere.

As he merged onto the Harbor Tunnel Thruway, he flooded with relief. He felt as if he was hovering atop the roof of the panel truck, wind ruffling through his hair, no longer bound by gravity or any other earthly ties.

60

John Mattingly pulled into the parking lot of the Taylor Gardens apartment complex. It looked to be about 50 years old, but in reasonably good shape. It was from back when they built these things with brick. He didn't see any gardens.

Colin had awoken just before they hit the exit for the Beltway off of 95. Under John's persistent prodding, Colin outlined the operation. He didn't volunteer anything, but John kept pressing. Colin said nothing about Ohtari or their encounter earlier that evening at 3Make. He was providing an outline, not a confession. He wouldn't confess to anything because he did nothing wrong. He'd invented something wonderful; something nobody had done before. Colin wouldn't accept condemnation. If he hadn't invented The Helix someone else would have. Maybe not as soon. Maybe not as beautiful. Maybe not as deadly. But someone would have come up with something similar.

Colin did not believe in the singular inventor: The person who came up with something all on their own, without any outside influences. As much as Colin believed in his unique design sensibility, he knew he wasn't alone in his invention. It wouldn't work without the Chinese team's battery innovation. Wouldn't work without the material breakthroughs from 3Make that Jimmy Chen refined. When Colin thought about it, 3Make was as responsible for The Helix and its potential for mass manufacturing as he and Jimmy. They could talk all they wanted about what their technology could do for the manufacturing landscape, all the promise of localization and just-in-time parts, lightweighting of assemblies to save fuel costs, and all the other potential advances in medical, industrial and architectural engineering, but they couldn't deny the hunger for guns. Colin didn't invent the demand; he was just feeding it.

John didn't know what to think. The raw scheme laid out by Colin sounded believable and could probably be verified by what was in the back of the panel truck, but Colin and Jimmy sounded incredibly naïve. John didn't know much about Mikhail, but he knew the dude was dead serious. Dead being an operative word, because you don't keep the company of guys like Brad Davenport without delivering harm to people who get in your way.

John also knew that once you got into the fold with people like Mikhail, you were in for life, or at least until they had no further use for you. It was like those motorcycle clubs in which you sign on for life. No resigning to spend more time with family or because you want to devote your life to the Lord. If they want you to stay, for whatever reason, you stay.

Colin denied that Jimmy was on the run and John thought that he better not be. Guys like Colin and Jimmy might think they can disappear, but John knew that they'd leave footprints everywhere, especially in the digital age. Hiding is just about impossible, unless you were an expert at it. These two guys were rank amateurs as far as John could tell.

In one glimmer of candor, Colin told John that he and Jimmy just wanted to be free to design and make great stuff. But to John it sounded like they already had that freedom at 3Make. And if they didn't find it there, they could find it at another company according to what John had read about the market for good engineers. The best ones could move from company to company, anywhere in the world, anytime they wanted. It sounded like freedom to John. More than he had. More than Colin and Jimmy would ever have as cogs in Mikhail's operation. Now on top of everything, Colin and Jimmy had to evade the law. Despite their business, that's something John and his family rarely had to do. They embraced the law, not evaded it. They collaborated with lawmakers and law enforcement. In many ways the law was their ally.

John pulled into a parking space and looked around, Colin slumped against the passenger side door. No panel truck. Maybe they'd arrived before Jimmy, which Colin said was likely because Jimmy couldn't do anything without his phone, not even find the place where they'd lived the past three years.

Colin keep gazing out the passenger window, staring into blank space like he was hoping something would swoop into the parking lot and take him out of this situation. John tapped him on the shoulder to get his attention.

"Looks like no Jimmy. We have some time, but it's running low for your boy. No use sitting out here in the parking lot like secret lovers. Let's go inside."

61

"Hey Goddess. Barrett just arrived with another guy I don't recognize. They're in the apartment now. I'm thinking they're waiting for Chen. If they leave before Chen gets here, I'll confront them. I had a GPS tracker with me and secured it on the car they were in. What's the word on Chen?"

"I'm directly on his tail now, Tone. What's that Supertramp song? 'Take the Long Way Home'? The boy doesn't have much of a sense of direction. If he gets his bearings, I'd say we're about 10 minutes away."

"Wouldn't take you for a Supertramp fan. Maybe The Trammps, but not Supertramp."

"Never heard of The Trammps. Supertramp is Joy's thing. You gotta plan, Tone?"

"I'm thinking we divide and conquer. You take care of Chen and I'll handle Barrett and the other guy."

"The other guy is a wild card. Probably from that house where they were hiding out. He might be a pro, Tone. You sure you want to go lonestar with those two? Remember, Barrett's likely the guy who did Ohtari with that Gucci ghost gun."

"Yeah, I know, Goddess, but I'm thinking I have the element of surprise at my disposition. I've also got my unique charm."

"No offense, Tone, but personality didn't help Ohtari."

"Offense taken. I'm to charm what Jeff Beck is to guitar."

"Who?"

"Never mind, I'm going to station myself outside the apartment. Stay sound, Goddess."

"You too, Tone."

62

Jimmy Chen was relieved to find his way to the apartment after seemingly driving around the entirety of Parkville. But the relief was short-lived. The moment he stepped down from the cab of the truck he heard his name called out. He turned around to see a tall Black woman. The cleaning woman!

"You're...who are you? What are you doing here?" The words rushed from his trembling lips.

"Nothing to worry about, Jimmy. I just need to talk with you."

"About what?"

"About what you're doing with that truck, among other things."

Jimmy looked wildly from side to side, paused for a moment, threw the truck keys into the shrubs in front of the apartment building, and took off across the parking lot toward a small wooded area.

"Ah, shit, Jimmy," Charlaine yelled, sprinting after him. Jimmy was quick at first but was slowing down even before he reached the edge of the lot. He entered the woods in a halting gallop, following a barely visible, narrow path. He was gasping for air, seemingly not able to draw enough oxygen to compensate for his heavy breathing. He reached a slight slope bending to the left, the path partially covered in pine straw. As he veered with the path, Jimmy slipped, falling hard on his left side. He could hear the Black woman's footsteps growing louder. As he scrambled to regain his feet, she called out to him.

"Jimmy, stop. Don't run. I just want to talk."

Her voice was calm, as if this was an everyday thing. Jimmy scrambled to a seated position and thrust his hand into the left pocket of his jacket, finding the grip of The Helix.

"No, Jimmy, don't even think about it. You're not in trouble yet, but you will be if you use that again."

Jimmy panicked when he heard the word "again."

He pulled the gun out of his pocket and pointed it at Charlaine's chest 10 feet away.

"Back off. Who are you and what do you want with me?"

Charlaine raised her hands and took a couple of steps back. Her Glock pressed against the small of her back.

"I'm an investigator working with 3Make, Jimmy. You're not in trouble. We just want to talk."

"I don't have anything to say," Jimmy wheezed, the adrenaline making his hand shake.

"Just put the gun away, Jimmy. I know you and Colin had a confrontation with Ohtari. He probably charged Colin and Colin fired on him. Or maybe you did. It was self-defense, right? You're no killer. But if you shoot me, you'll be hunted and caught, I guarantee. And put away for a long, long time. Quit now while you're ahead. Just slide the gun toward me. Gently, Jimmy, gently."

Her voice felt like a blanket to Jimmy, soothing his shaking body. He exhaled and suddenly felt as if every bit of energy had rushed from his body, leaving him limp and deflated. His grip on The Helix weakened and he saw the gun drop at his feet.

"Okay, Jimmy. That's good. Stay there and I'll help you up. Get you something to drink."

Jimmy sunk back, the back of his head hitting the ground with a thud. The jolt to his head sent a new wave of fear through his body. As Charlaine walked slowly toward him, hands still up, Jimmy grabbed the gun and told her to stop. She did as she was told and he pointed the gun at her from the sitting position. He looked at it for a moment as if he was examining it for purchase, turned it toward his face and fired a moment before Charlaine fell on top of him.

The thin bullet went straight through his right eye socket and out the back of his head, splintering the trunk of a pine tree before burrowing into the soft earth. Charlaine pushed herself off of Jimmy and turned her head from the hole in his eye socket. She stood up, pulled off her jacket, brushed it off, and draped it gently over Jimmy's head and upper body, being careful not to look at his right eye. As she began walking back through the woods, she saw a tall man run to his car, start it up, and squeal out of the apartment complex. She broke out in a sprint toward the landing outside Colin and Jimmy's apartment.

63

Tony heard Charlaine yell at Jimmy, but held his position at the second-floor landing outside Colin and Jimmy's apartment. His first instinct was to run to Charlaine's aid, but he knew that Jimmy wouldn't get far.

Charlaine ran the 440-yard dash in high school, and although she wasn't in competitive shape, she could outrun anyone Tony knew. He'd had a candidate for an opening at DII who claimed he was second in the state in the 100 meters hurdle in high school and could chase down anyone. Tony listened slightly amused and asked him if he thought he could beat Charlaine in a race down the block. Charlaine was dressed in undercover mode, in those floppy sweats and Skechers. She didn't look particularly athletic, until she blew by the guy 10 yards into the race and coasted comfortably in front of him to the end of the block. Tony went up to the guy, shook his hand, thanked him for his time, and told him he was impressive but not a good fit. Tony hated people who exaggerated their capabilities. Those kind of people can put others in deadly situations.

Tony got out his phone to text Charlaine when the apartment door opened and out stepped Colin with the bigger guy following him. Colin was holding a two-handled joystick and a paper bag. He stopped in his tracks when he saw Tony blocking the stairs, looking like an offensive lineman daring a linebacker to rush. The other guy tugged on Colin's arm, but Colin stayed cemented in place.

"Colin Barrett?" Tony's voice was light but strong, with an authority that was chilling to Colin.

"Who wants to know?" asked John tentatively. John could be considered part of the criminal element, but nobody mistook him for a tough guy. He had a gun but had never pointed it at anyone. Even so, he started to inch his hand toward his right front pocket.

"No, please don't reach for anything. It wouldn't be a good idea for you or Colin," Tony said softly, as he pulled his Sig Sauer 9mm micro compact from the holster beneath his loose sweatshirt. "I don't know what your connection is to Colin, but it's best you steer clear."

"I'd be leaving right now if you weren't bogarting the stairwell."

"Okay, I'll think about letting you go, but first take that piece out of your pocket, lay it on the ground, and push it over to me. Slowly, gently, like you're sliding a fresh beer across the bar."

John reached in his pocket, felt the handle of the gun, eased it out with his thumb and index finger, stooped down and slowly placed it on the concrete landing, keeping his hand on it a second before releasing it from his grasp. He hovered his hand above the gun for a second or two before swiftly kicking it as hard as he could between Tony's legs. As Tony looked down at the gun careening toward him, John leaped to his right, vaulted over the stair railing, and sprinted down the steps.

Tony turned to follow him, but then jerked his torso back in Colin's direction. Colin stood in the same spot in a daze, unable to move. Tony took a few steps down the stairs and recovered the other guy's gun, putting it in his pocket. He heard a car screech out of the parking lot and smiled, remembering that he'd put the GPS tracker on the car. Tony turned back toward Colin, took a deep breath and addressed him in a priestly voice.

"Okay, Colin, are we cool? You don't have one of those ghost guns, do you?"

Colin's face reddened.

"It's not a piece-of-shit ghost gun. Don't ever call it that."

Tony looked at Colin, the pride of ownership evident in his defiance, and nodded his head.

"Okay, I'll never call it that again. I'm sorry to have offended. What do you call it, Colin?"

Colin looked down, slightly embarrassed by his outburst, and whispered.

"I call it The Helix. And I don't have one on me or you'd be dead by now."

Tony sighed and walked with small, halting steps toward Colin.

"Okay, I'm going to escort you back to the apartment where we can talk. Are you cool?"

Colin shrugged his shoulders.

"Yeah, I'm good. I was just trying to get this stuff to Jimmy, that's all."

"Okay, no worries, hand over your keys. Your friend Jimmy should be joining us shortly."

64

Charlaine and Tony sat across from one another at a diner on Boston Street between Fells Point and Canton. It was 4 a.m. and business was slow after the bars had emptied and before the breakfast crowd. Charlaine and Tony had spent the last two hours selectively recounting the night's events to various law enforcement teams.

Charlaine took a sip of tepid coffee and gazed at Tony with sagging eyes.

"You shoulda let me have the two guys and you taken Chen, Tone."

"How so?" Tony yawned and stirred his coffee. He wouldn't get to bed tonight. He'd have a few fingers of Elijah Craig and do what he called a renumeration of the day's events.

"Chen wouldn't have run on you. He woulda stood down. He still saw me as that cleaning woman. Thought a no-running sucker like himself could escape from me. He'd be alive now if it was you instead of me."

"You don't think Colin and the other dude would have tested you?"

"Oh, definitely, but they would have done it from the get-go. They wouldn't have fooled me into thinking they'd hand themselves over to me. I'd have been on guard. You'd have used that voice of authority to make Chen surrender himself to you."

"And yet, Goddess, I let this guy distract me by kicking a gun under my legs, even though I already had a gun on him. I mean, me, Tony Mancuso, going for that kind of second-rate move? I'm embarrassed up to my cauliflower ears, Goddess. But, we live and learn, and the first participle is the most important one."

"Leave it to you to put things in perspective, Tony. First time I've heard you speak of yourself in the third person. A little tip: Don't use it on Lidia. Or anybody else for that matter. We fucked up. Not you; we. I had no idea guys like Barrett and Chen existed. And I, we Tone, should have known. They're not be-true-to-your-school, straight-laced, for-the-good-of-everyone people. They're not clichés. Not nerds. They've got their own fucked up shit. I should know better than to stereotype anyone, having been confronted with that shit all my life."

Tony nodded.

"There's an onerous of truth in what you say, Goddess. I was guilty of the thing I warn everybody against: assuming. Assuming these guys were harmless eggheads."

"One other thing, Tone. We shoulda took what we knew when we knew it to the cops. We might have saved a life. You ever think of hubris?"

"You mean that Middle Eastern stuff they put on pita bread?" Tony paused for a bit, a rueful smile on his face. "Yeah, I know it, Godly One, and I think I'm full of it."

Epilogue

The police search of the Mattingly property in Anne Arundel County didn't uncover any illegal firearms. The officers enjoyed a nice post-search plate of barbecue, potato salad, hush puppies and coleslaw, along with a few glasses of the Mattingly's locally renowned whisky.

***

The boxes from the panel truck and the design files for The Helix were confiscated and handed over to the Defense Advanced Research Projects Agency (DARPA), where they are being analyzed for future use by the U.S. military. Colin Barrett and Roland Hines are unpaid consultants for the project.

***

Colin Barrett never faced trial for his alleged crimes. The Board at 3Make decided not to press charges, wary of bad publicity and thinking punishment for Barrett would serve no good purpose. Colin pleaded with 3Make to get his job back, and the new chief technology officer, Roland Hines, granted him his wish with the Board's approval. On the surface, nothing had changed with Colin: same job, same apartment, same quiet demeanor. But Roland saw something different. He called it gravitas; a sense of seriousness about his work and his commitment to the company that gave him a second chance. In quiet moments, Colin harbored regrets for the first time. He was complicit in two deaths and the disappearance of Bill Christenson. He held secrets that could explode at any moment:

The knowledge that Mikhail was still watching his every move, and that his design for The Helix resided on a Russian server, likely waiting for another Chen to bring it to fruition. Roland sensed the new vulnerability in Colin and acted as a surrogate father, giving the younger man a life outside of work for the first time.

***

No one was charged for the shooting of Spencer Ohtari. There was no witness except for Barrett, the purported shooter was dead, and the body was not found. The world was short on sympathy for Ohtari. Two women were in the process of filing sexual assault charges against him at the time of his death. It seemed as if everybody, including his ex-wife, his two adult children, and a few past girlfriends, thought the world was a better place without Ohtari.

***

Jimmy Chen's death was ruled a suicide. He was never memorialized. Roland Hines visited Jimmy's parents and sister after his death and told them about the materials he developed and how they would be used around the world for a new generation of products. He didn't mention The Helix. Jimmy's father was bewildered at his son's plight, while his mother and sister accepted it as fate, never considering why the fickle finger pointed at Jimmy. Colin Barrett is the one person who misses Jimmy every day. He keeps Jimmy's game controller on the mantelpiece in his apartment, talking to it when he gets lonely or scared.

***

The man named Mikhail reluctantly left his condo in Jacksonville Beach as a precaution and moved to a house on the lake in the western part of South Carolina. True to his word, Barrett was no snitch, saying nothing about the Mikhail connection. Mikhail is currently intrigued about the black market for 3D-printed replacement limbs and organs in Asia and Africa.

***

After arriving Sunday night to a vacant house, with her husband's closet missing some of his clothes and a suitcase, and his truck, trailer and boat missing from the garage, Tracey Christenson initially thought her husband had skipped out on her. But, she thought if he was that upset, he would have left a note, or a text, or an email. No money was missing from their banking or investment accounts. When he didn't show up at home or work on Monday, she filed a missing person's report. At Bernard Jamal's suggestion, Tracey also hired DII to look into her husband's disappearance. Charlaine Pennington is currently on the case, looking into a tip from a couple who were fishing by the side of the reservoir when Bill Christenson's boat headed toward the landing on a late Friday afternoon. They'd talked with Bill a few times while fishing at Pretty Boy, and had marveled at the coincidence that all three graduated from NC State University, home of the Wolfpack. So, they were surprised when Bill didn't return the Wolfpack sign when they flashed it in greeting as he was motoring toward the landing.

***

Brad Davenport, who goes by David Pearson in his hometown, pulled into the marina and bait shop on the Nansemond River in a Ford F-150 XL truck pulling a trailer with a boat on top. The truck and boat looked freshly painted. He was there for his morning coffee with Peggy Dunseth, who runs the facility for her father. David is working part time as a guide for fisherman unfamiliar with the local waters. He also does routine maintenance for the marina and shop. He and Peggy don't talk much, being comfortable with long periods of silence. When they do speak, it's about the weather, tides, fishing conditions, or the latest episode of "Better Call Saul." Peggy is a widow, and thinks David might have potential. David has no romantic illusions, but he feels good helping somebody out. Maybe if he keeps it up, it will wipe out those shining eyes he keeps seeing in his sleep.

***

Jackie Reynolds did his three months in rehab and then spent another nine months working in the facility's kitchen, where his Saturday gumbo was a big hit. Joe Monroe visited him once a week, sometimes bringing him crab cake po'boys like his wife used to make. At the end of his 12-month stint at No Fear, Jackie worked up a proposal for a food truck called Engagin' Cajun. It is the first non-technology investment that Bernard Jamal has greenlighted.

***

Buck Boyd was working his usual spot at the end of the bar in Essex early one Friday night when a stocky Italian guy took the stool next to him. The guy looked to be in his early 50s and Buck had never seen him in the bar. He addressed Buck by name, and when Buck didn't respond, he clenched his fist under the bar and delivered a short, but powerful right fist into Buck's groin. As Buck doubled over in pain, the guy whispered in his ear, "That was for Bernard Jamal, who's nine times the man you are. If I see you anywhere I don't think you should be, there's more where that came from." While Buck writhed in pain, the guy got up from the stool, left a $20 on the bar, and walked calmly out the door, humming Dion's "The Wanderer."

***

Charlaine found the young woman she called Little Lucy working in a ramshackle bar in the area where Curtis Bay bleeds into Brooklyn. Charlaine was going to mete out some revenge when she saw the men clawing over the small redhead and leaving only spare change as tips. Charlaine thought of Bernard Jamal's generosity toward Jackie Reynolds and the animosity drained from her body. She gave her card to the woman named Ashley, and told her she would help her get into rehab and go back to school. Ashley never called. Five months later she was dead from a fentanyl overdose.

***

Nine months after the abduction attempt, Bernard Jamal and Kensey Mathers married in a civil ceremony at the Baltimore City Courthouse, witnessed by their mutual friend John Summers. Kensey took the job at Scan2CAD, where, thanks to management's enlightened stance toward employees, she works a 35-hour week. Bernard is still plying the VC trade, trying to find the next big thing, which he thinks might be 3D-printed housing. He and Summers still dominate the Thursday night pickup games at Farley Recreation Center.

***

Tony Mancuso vowed to cut back on his hours and brought in an office manager and two new investigators to help with the DII case load. He's become more careful about the jobs he accepts and he brings in the police earlier and more often in his cases. He and Lidia take long weekends at their place in Ocean City six times a year and rent it out the rest of the time to offset the ownership costs. Bernard Jamal helped Carmelo develop a better left-handed dribble and now he's only stripped of the ball every third time up the court.

***

Two months after the 3Make case, a blonde miniature poodle named Shirley came into Charlaine and Joy's life. Joy picked her out from a local shelter. Charlaine thought it was typical of Joy to up the ante by not just selecting an older dog, but one that was blind and suffered from extreme separation anxiety. None of those drawbacks ended up being a problem. The dog has some kind of secret sense that makes up for her lack of sight, leaping up on the arm of the sofa, walking across it like a tightrope, and plopping to the floor on soft feet. Separation anxiety is rarely an issue, as Charlaine and Joy suffer from the same affliction. Although Joy spends more time with the poodle and takes care of most of its needs, Shirley is more attached to Charlaine. It's as if the dog senses who needs more comforting and applies her attention accordingly.

***

Joe Monroe is 50,000 words into his first crime novel, tentatively titled "Curtis Bay Blues."

***

Acknowledgments

Many people contributed to this book through their encouragement and good faith in the author, but several went beyond the call of duty with their discerning reading, technical advice, and healthy criticism. They are Rachael Dalton-Taggart, John Kelly, Ruth Pritchard-Kelly, Mike Poletynski, Leah Thayer, Deelip Menezes, Dave Cothran, and John Cramblitt. Thanks, as always, to my wife Peggy Kelly, whose unflagging belief and patience got me through the rough days and nights of rewrites, proofing and reproofing. The author takes sole responsibility for factual, grammatical, continuity, typographical or other errors.

About the Author

After a 40-year career as a communications manager, PR specialist, and writer for digital technology companies, R.A. Cramblitt has transitioned to fiction in its myriad forms. His first novel, *Probably Lives in Tahiti,* earned a 4.8-star rating on Amazon and a 4.76-star rating on Goodreads. *The Parker Chronicles*, a 2021 collection of vignettes on the vagaries of everyday life, also earned 4.8 stars on Amazon. Cramblitt's short story, "Long Live Lenny Leftover" was published in issue 10 of the Waxing and Waning Literary Journal.